No

Fury

A Montague and Strong Detective Agency Novel

By

Orlando A. Sanchez

Victorious warriors win first and then go to war, while defeated warriors go to war first and then seek to win.—Sun Tzu

Keep your friends close, but your enemies closer. —Machiavelli

Ode to an Agency

I tell you a tale from the land of the free

Of Montague and Strong Detective Agency

Simon is Strong and good for a laugh

Kali has marked him so there'll be no epitaph

Graced with immortality can still be a bane,

When his partner is worried re: the state of his brain.

Tristan is Monty, long-suffering and brave,

Though with his mageness can seem morbidly grave.

He wiggles his fingers and lo and behold

Magic reveals that the glitter's not necessarily gold

Demons and Demigods and Dragons abound

Our heroes resilience never fails to astound

Our duo have Peaches that you shouldn't bite

For he is a hellhound who's good in a fight

He considers sausage a good start to the day

How many he devours is rather difficult to say.

For Simon, his poison is Death Wish coffee

While Monty can't Mage before a good cup of tea

I don't need liquid brew, sayeth Peaches, Meat is Life!

It helps my saliva get you both out of

strife.

-Carrie Anne O’Leary

This is a work of fiction. All of the characters, organizations, and events portrayed in this novel are either products of the author's imagination or are used fictitiously and are not to be construed as real. Any resemblance to actual events, locales, organizations, or persons, living or dead, is entirely coincidental.

Published by Bitten Peaches Publishing NY NY

Cover Design by Deranged Doctor Design
www.derangeddoctordesign.com

ONE

"WHAT DO YOU mean, kidnapped?" I asked.

Corbel reached into a pocket and produced two medium-sized sausages. He tossed one to Peaches, who caught and inhaled it in one bite.

<Why didn't you let me know he was there? I almost shot him.>

<He isn't a bad man. He smells like home and he has meat.>

"He's getting big." Corbel rubbed Peaches' head, as my Hellhound chomped on the second sausage he fed him.

"Who would kidnap Hades' wife?"

Corbel stared at me. "That's the first intelligent question you've asked," he said, rubbing his face. "I don't know who would be suicidal enough to make this move against Hades."

"Where was she?" Monty asked. "You said she never made it to her scheduled pick up. Pick up from where?"

"At her home."

"Not the Underworld?" I asked. "Isn't that where she

lives?"

"Persephone spends a large portion of her time on this plane," Corbel answered. "Their relationship is *complex*."

"She has a home here?" Monty asked. "In the city?"

Corbel nodded. "Midtown, off Central Park West. The Eldorado."

"Does anyone know where this alleged kidnapping took place?" I asked. "Was she home?"

"No, security is too tight," Corbel said with a shake of his head. "What do you mean *alleged*? She was taken."

"Have you met Hades?" I said, giving a short laugh. "He is the god of the Underworld —not exactly Mr. Cheerful and Romance. Maybe she wanted something different in her life. Maybe a place with a little sun?"

"Are you implying she *left* him?" Corbel said more than asked. He flexed his jaw. "She would *never* leave him."

"*Wouldn't* leave him, or *can't* leave him?" I asked, wiggling my fingers. "Maybe Hades worked some spell on her."

"Their relationship is *complex*," Corbel said again with a sigh. "No, she wasn't compelled to remain with him."

"Complex? Is that code for she can't stand him?"

"Complex," he said, glaring at me. "Like the kind of relationship an immortal detective might have with an ancient vampire."

"Ouch, no need to get sensitive. Just asking the basic questions."

"If you ask those questions, prepare for pain."

"Just noting that they spent time apart," I answered.

"Did she care for him?"

Corbel glared at me again. "She and Hades have an understanding. They take regular time away from each other."

"Does he love her? Or does he go around Zeusafying every woman he sees, making little demigods?"

"He loves her," Corbel said with finality. "He wouldn't subject me to the torture of speaking to you if he didn't."

I nodded. "Right, so she was kidnapped, or she ran away."

"For your self-preservation, I'm going to suggest you refrain from expressing that opinion around Hades when you meet him."

"Meet him? We *literally* just got home. Can you give us a moment to at least change clothes?"

"No. Hades wants you on this now."

"Before we go to see your boss, we should see her place," I said. "Maybe there's something there that will let us know who's behind this. Maybe a boyfriend?"

Corbel shook his head and looked at Monty. "How do you work with him?"

"Tea and patience," Monty said, "copious amounts of both."

TWO

WE DROVE TO The Eldorado, and I parked the Dark Goat in front of the entrance. The building dated back to the early 1900s, and was one of the more elegant and iconic properties facing the park. I looked around and noticed something missing that surprised me.

"Don't these buildings usually have door attendants or people-greeters?" I asked, looking around. "I thought living in the swanky Upper West Side meant you didn't have to open your own doors?"

"It also usually means," Monty started, "not having cursed automobiles that exude an undercurrent of fear or Hellhound creatures near your building,"

"I think I see our man," I said, looking at the entrance. "What is he doing?"

Monty raised an eyebrow, adjusted his sleeves, and looked at the entrance. Just inside the foyer stood a man in uniform. I could tell from the look on his face that he was considering making this his last morning on the job and ducking out the service entrance.

"I'm pretty certain that look is called self-preservation," Monty said after a few seconds. "He's probably considering retirement at this moment."

Corbel cleared his throat and waved from the back seat. A flicker of recognition crossed the door attendant's face, and he relaxed just enough to get a grip. Judging from his facial expression, the hold on his flagging courage was slippery at best.

"Your car is scaring Howard witless," Corbel said. "Either that or he got a look at your Hellhound."

Corbel managed to slide over and claim more of the back seat. In a surprising display of generosity, Peaches reduced his sprawl by several inches.

<Nice of you to let him have some room.>

<He smells like home, and he gave me meat. I will share my seat with him.>

"His name is Peaches, not Hellhound," I said, irritated. "Just like your name is Corbel, not butthead. One is a name. The other is what he is."

"Hilarious," Corbel replied. "Either way, this car is inducing some serious fear."

"It's a feature," I answered. "You should see what it can do when Monty really cuts loose with the mayhem and destruction."

Monty glared in my direction. "I do no such thing."

"Cecil runed this with—what?" Corbel asked, examining the interior. "Obliteration runes?"

"Why aren't you affected like Howard over there?" I asked. "Monty and I are keyed to the Dark Goat, but you are—"

"The Hound of Hades," Corbel answered, with an edge to his voice. I noticed his jaw muscles flexing for a moment, then he took a deep breath. "Do you really think the runes in this car would affect me?"

"Merely making an observation," I said. "You, unlike Howard, aren't about to run for the hills."

I was also trying to find out if Corbel had any major weaknesses. It wasn't like he was going to say: 'By the way, green vegetables are my greatest weakness, which is why I never eat them.' Although, if I fed some to Peaches, the deathane could probably level a city block.

Today's friend is tomorrow's enemy, and Corbel worked for Hades—so far, the scariest of the gods I'd met, besides Chaos. Hades wasn't the 'all in your face explosion and death' scary. Hades was the subtle, calculating, Kasparov- seeing-one-hundred-moves-ahead kind of scary. I'd take the explosive scary any day.

Hades never did anything without a motive and purpose. Even the gift of Peaches, I knew, came with some kind of condition. This case was about as fun as running naked and blindfolded through a minefield. I didn't trust Hades, and I didn't trust his Hound.

"Is there any way to reduce the intensity of the runes?" Corbel asked, looking at Howard. "The man looks like he wants to bolt."

"Sure," I said, reaching under the dashboard. "I'm sure Cecil installed a dial somewhere so we could go from 'mind-numbing scared shitless' to 'butterflies in your stomach.' Just give me a second, so I can find it."

"How can you always be this irritating?" Corbel asked, staring at me through the rear-view mirror. "How have you managed to live this—nevermind."

"Years and years of practice, Mr. Hound," I said. "This advanced level of snark fu is only attained by the most diligent of students."

"Snark fu?" Corbel asked. "What the—?"

"Don't encourage him," Monty interrupted, opening his door. "Let's see if we can calm down the doorman and investigate the premises."

The door attendant opened the main door, a look of fear gripping his features as he approached. He actually made it pretty close to the car, stopping mid-sidewalk before reconsidering. I gave him extra points for the attempt.

It wasn't that the Dark Goat was scary…per se.

Cecil, the owner of SuNaTran, went slightly overboard with his latest edition.

SuNaTran provided discreet service any time of day or night to any of the five boroughs and beyond—for a price. The transportation they provided was the height of security, but there was a problem. The vehicles no longer appeared secure.

It was Monty's fault.

The Dark Goat was a SuNaTran work of runic automotive art. A remodeled and runed 1967 Pontiac GTO in black, with highlights of purple that shifted to black. The height of American muscle, combined with the safeguards of the present. The Dark Goat, like all SuNaTran vehicles, was a small tank disguised as a car.

The Pontiac GTO got its name from the Ferrari 250 GTO, a rare and beautiful piece of automotive art. The GTO stood for Grand Tourismo Omologato. I'm sure no one wanted to say that mouthful—so GTO became the Goat, and a legendary muscle car was christened.

The Dark Goat was intentionally cursed. Cecil was having a bit of a PR problem with SuNaTran, mostly due to Monty and his violent friends. The last Goat, may it rest in pieces, was reduced to slag by a Ghost Magistrate.

I had taken a SuNaTran Lamborghini Aventador on a date. A troll had decided it would be better in small parts and attached a bomb to it, rendering it into Aventador art. It wasn't the only casualty of my date that night.

Cecil was still pissed off about that.

After what happened to the last SuNaTran vehicle, a Lamborghini Urus we had while in London, I could understand Cecil's reluctance in providing us with transportation. SuNaTran's reputation was taking a hit, and he felt we owed him our assistance in restoring the company's tarnished name, considering we were the ones doing the tarnishing.

Enter the Dark Goat.

There was a method to his madness. The runes that cursed the Dark Goat were taken from another, darker, vehicle—a 1970 Chevy Camaro dubbed the Beast. That thing killed its drivers. Something to do with the runic configuration and its disruption of life energies.

I never did ask where Cecil got the runes for the Beast, and Monty wasn't sharing. Something told me I didn't want to know their origin.

Cecil had tried, and failed, to destroy the Beast several times. From what Monty told me, the Night Warden, Grey Stryker or Schneider something or another, had a connection to the cursed vehicle. He was driving the Beast. He wasn't immortal, but he was the only driver to survive that thing.

It was a win-win situation for Cecil. If we destroyed the Dark Goat, he would learn how to destroy the

Beast, provided we survived whatever destroyed the Goat. If the Dark Goat withstood our use, Cecil could point to us and promote how awesome SuNaTran vehicles were.

Most of the time, people had a visceral reaction to the inherent danger of standing next to, or riding in, the Dark Goat. It felt mean and angry. It triggered a reaction in your limbic brain. There was no fight, flight, or freeze—with the Dark Goat, it was all flight.

I loved the Dark Goat.

The expression on the door attendant's face went from startled to terror as he backed up to the entrance of the building. I got out and opened the suicide door, letting Peaches out. I looked down at my overgrown canine as the suspension of the Dark Goat rocked and creaked, begging for mercy as he bounded onto the sidewalk.

<If we aren't going to change your diet, I'm going to put you on an exercise program.>

<No more healthy sausage?>

I remembered the deathane with a shudder.

<It's not safe for anyone to have you eat healthy sausage. You'll need to exercise.>

<An exercise program? Does this program have meat?>

<No. It doesn't. At this point, I'm going to have to feed you entire cows. Something has to give.>

<Something is giving entire cows? Can we go there next?>

I shook my head as we followed Corbel to the entrance of the building. The Eldorado was an art deco masterpiece and part of the Central Park West Historic District. The lobby of The Eldorado was a combination of dark and light green marble with wood accents.

Several seating areas held large sofas and were designed in the cavernous style of old New York, when there was a race to be the tallest and most opulent.

Howard took refuge behind an enormous wooden reception desk at the far end of the lobby. The elevator banks were behind the reception desk.

"What floor does Mrs. Hades live on?"

"Her name is Persephone, not Mrs. Hades," Corbel answered. "Don't you study at all?"

"Of course," I said. "They did a great job in that movie when she was running things with the Merovingian."

"The Merovin—?" Corbel started.

"Then Morpheus and crew show up and—"

"That's not even remotely close," Corbel said, flexing his jaw again. "This is not a movie, and she's not running things with a Merovingian. Do you even know who they were?"

"The sons of Merovech," Monty said. "Most of Gaul was united under one of his sons, Clovis."

Corbel and I both stared at Monty.

"Really?" I asked. "Clovis?"

"It's called study," Monty said, "mages do it occasionally."

"You may want to consider it, Strong," Corbel said. "Might actually help you learn something."

"Oh, the hilarity astounds," I retorted. "So, Mrs. Hades lived where exactly?"

"Lives, she's not dead, Strong, just missing," Corbel answered with a growl. "Her home is in the South Tower. Thirtieth floor."

Howard appeared to retreat, shrinking behind the reception desk as we approached. I placed a hand on Peaches' head.

<*He looks scared. I don't want an incident, keep the growl low.*>

<*Can I just smile at him?*>

Hellhounds can do many things, smiling wasn't one of them.

<*Of course. It's always friendly to smile at door attendants and reception personnel. Don't forget the low growl.*>

<*Do you think he has meat?*>

<*Anything is possible. Remember, big smile, low growl.*>

THREE

WE STOPPED SEVERAL feet away from Howard's barricade of a desk, and let Corbel approach. A few things happen when a Hellhound attempts to smile, none of it pretty. He bares his teeth and gives the impression that ripping off your leg and snacking on it is imminent.

"What is wrong with *your* creature?" Monty said under his breath next to me. "Is he trying to give the doorman a heart attack?"

"He's being friendly," I said, patting Peaches' head. "He's practicing his smile. What do you think?"

Monty glanced down at the 'smiling' Peaches.

"I think his lack of lips is deterring the process," Monty said. "Have him stop before we need to rush the doorman to the hospital."

"I think it's actually getting better," I said. "His first smile" —I shook my head— "now *that* needed work."

"You seem to get a perverse joy out of tormenting door attendants with your creature," Monty answered. "Why not train him to eat *less*?"

"Now you're just talking crazy," I said as Corbel approached. "The new plan is to have him exercise more."

"Well, he can hardly exercise any less," Monty said. "He barely moves as it is, unless meat is involved."

Corbel cleared his throat.

"Howard is going to unlock the penthouse access, but he won't ride in the same elevator with *Peaches*," Corbel said, looking down at my Hellhound. "We'll have to wait until he gets up there."

"Thank you," I said with a nod. "See, old hounds *can* be taught new tricks."

"One thing," Corbel added, as we waited for the elevator. "This building is a landmark."

I glanced over at him.

"Thanks—I guess," I said. "I know the building is old" —I looked around— "I didn't realize you were on the Landmark Commission. Amazing use of art deco design elements, though. I didn't know you were into architecture?"

"Don't be dense," Corbel said as the elevator arrived. "Hades owns the apartment Persephone uses. Anything happens here, it gets back to Terra Sur, the company he owns."

"I don't understand what you're getting at," I said. "What does that have to do with—?"

"You two," Corbel said, stepping into the elevator and pointing at Monty and me, "have a particular set of skills."

"You must have me confused with—" I started.

"No," Corbel said, his voice hard. "Do *not* destroy this building."

"Destroy?" I asked. "We're just going to check Mrs. Hades' apartment. How much destruction can *that* cause?"

Monty gave a sage nod. "I don't foresee any difficulty inspecting the premises," Monty said. "This is a routine procedure."

An audible creaking greeted us as Peaches stepped onto the elevator. I looked down at my slightly rotund Hellhound. Peaches proceeded to look away, suddenly interested in the floor, as the elevator doors closed with a sigh and a ding.

Corbel rubbed his face with a sigh as we started ascending.

"I'm going to keep saying this until you understand it, Strong, seeing as how you are the denser of the two," Corbel answered as we arrived at the top floor. "We leave this building the same way we found it—intact."

"You know," I said, looking around the elevator, "many of these older buildings, especially the landmarks, need renovations, and are full of code violations. Usually the city is only a few days away from shutting them down—just saying."

Corbel glared at me. "Intact. I mean it."

FOUR

WE STEPPED OFF the elevator and onto the first-floor landing of a dual-terraced triplex penthouse. The first thing I noticed were the runes. Every surface of the landing, floor to ceiling, contained some kind of symbol.

"Hades takes this security thing seriously," I said, trying to decipher some of the runes on the wall next to the elevator. "I can't make out most of these. By most, I mean any."

Corbel stared at me. "You think?" he asked. "His wife lives here for six months of the year."

"These runes look dangerous," I said, still examining some of the symbols. "Fearsome, but not very effective if she was taken from here."

"We don't think this was the point of capture," Corbel answered. "Too difficult and too exposed."

"Indeed," Monty said. "Persephone is not entirely powerless either. Can you decipher these?"

Corbel pointed to a particular grouping of symbols.

"These mean protection," Corbel said, looking

farther down the wall and pointing, "and these are usually translated as: immense pain to the destroyers of old edifices."

"Good one," I said, looking at Monty. "I think you mean it reads: pain to the angry flinger of magic."

Monty stepped closer to the runes.

"These aren't normal runes, these are proto-runes," he said, narrowing his eyes. "I can just barely make out the meanings."

Corbel shook his head. "Of course they're proto-runes," he said and waved his hand in the air in front of him. "Did you think Hades would use normal runes? He's a god."

"These are even older than the lost runes," Monty said with a trace of awe in his voice as he took in the hallway. "The energy contained in the hallway alone—"

"Can reduce us to dust," Corbel replied, motioning forward with his chin. A path of runes illuminated the hallway in front of us. "Stay on the path until we get inside."

"What happens if we step off of it?" I asked, making sure my feet remained well within the path as we approached the door to the penthouse proper. "Do we set off an alarm?"

"You'll get to test your immortality and see if you can return from dust particles." Corbel glanced at me. "That's *all* that will be left of you."

"Ouch," I muttered under my breath. "Right, so keep feet on the path."

Peaches nudged my leg and nearly sent me to an instant dusting.

<You need to learn your strength.>

<I know my strength. I'm very strong.>

I decided to let that one go. Unless Peaches was in XL mode, our conversations usually had a singular focus…meat.

<What do you want? I mean, besides knocking my hip out of its socket?>

<Do you think he has more meat?>

<You just ate. Even if he did, I don't think you should eat so soon.>

<Why not?>

<Because I don't want you falling through the floor.>

<Are you saying I'm heavy?>

<I'm not saying it. The Dark Goat being barely able to hold you is saying it. Along with the elevator, which creaked and squealed all the way up to this floor.>

<Both those things are old. That is why they make noise. Like you in the morning when you wake up.>

<Age is not the point. Your weight is.>

<I'm hungry. The cold girl said I'm a puppy, and puppies need to eat all the time.>

<Puppy? Since when is Cecelia a Hellhound expert?>

<Since we saved you from Murk.>

<First, thank you. Second, that doesn't make you or any of your Coo coo ca choo friends experts in anything, except almost getting yourselves killed.>

<We were perfectly safe. We had a guardian, the beautiful Rags.>

I shook my head slowly.

<You were minutes away from losing it. You know I'm right.>

<I didn't lose you.>

I didn't know what to say to that. He was right.

Peaches and his menagerie of friends had found—and rescued—me.

<Frank said you would 'flake' with the meat, but I don't see any meat peeling off your body.>

<I don't want you hanging out with that lizard. He's a bad influence.>

<He's a dragon, not a lizard. He doesn't like to be called a lizard.>

<He's no dragon except in his imagination. I've met dragons, and that little lizard is not a dragon.>

<Is that the same way you aren't a mage?>

<Something like that. I want you to stay away from him.>

<He's my friend. Frank says you owe me a lifetime supply of sausages on demand because we saved you.>

<Frank and I are going to have a serious conversation.>

<The same way the angry man has conversations?>

<That's going to depend on the lizard.>

We had reached the entrance to Persephone's apartment. Corbel placed a hand on the door, and the runes shifted around the surface.

"Runic combination?" Monty asked. "Who else had this combination?"

"Hades, Persephone, and myself," Corbel said. "I would maintain and use the property when Persephone was with Hades."

Corbel stepped into the space, with Monty trailing behind him.

<It's not Coo coo ca choo.>

<What?>

<Our name. It's not Coo coo ca choo. It's Brew and Chew>

<Really? They are both equally bad.>

<No. Only one is the real name. You told me names have

power. The real name is Brew and Chew.>

<*I apologize. You're right. Names have power. I don't want you on any more Brew and Chew adventures if Frank is going to be part of this gang. He's bad news.*>

<*It's not a gang. It's a pack. Like you, the angry man, the old man with the bird, the scary lady, and the nice man.*>

<*Let's discuss this later.*>

<*After you get some meat?*>

<*After we find Mrs. Hades.*>

He sat on his haunches and looked up at me, remaining immobile. Monty poked his head outside.

"Are you guarding the landing?" Monty asked. "Or would you like to come in and, oh, I don't know, look for actual clues?"

I raised a finger.

<*And after we get some meat, fine.*>

<*Frank said that would work. See? He's not a bad influence.*>

My Hellhound padded inside as I stared after him.

"Discipline problem with the creature?" Monty asked, tracking Peaches as the Hellhound stepped past him.

"The little lizard is trying to corrupt my Hellhound," I said. "When I catch up to him, I'm going to squa—"

"Stay away from Frank and the Dive, Simon," Monty warned. "Night Wardens are an unstable bunch. Best to leave them, and their lizard dragons, alone."

"But he's trying to….I mean—" I started.

"Your creature is a *Hellhound*," Monty replied. "What harm could a *lizard* pose to him?"

"None," I answered.

"Precisely," Monty said, resting a hand on my

shoulder and ushering me into the apartment. "Now, let's go and find Persephone."

FIVE

I HEADED PAST the entrance, taken in by the décor. Persephone's triplex was impressive. Several staircases led to the second and third levels. The style was minimalist in earth tones with a hint of Asian influences.

Several of the art pieces I saw hanging around the space cost more than our entire place in The Moscow. On the walls, I noticed a few Picassos and Dalis. I doubted they were reprints.

Bloodwood floors glistened with a dull shine, and I saw many of the same runic symbols from the hallway spread out over the floor and walls. I was about to enter the cavernous living room when I felt the shift.

"Something feels off," I said, turning to Monty, who was currently airborne and forcefully exiting the apartment. I saw him crash into the wall in the hallway and fall to one knee.

"What…gave you that impression?" Monty said with a grunt, looking at me. "You have incoming."

I turned in time to leap away from a Hellhound

missile, as Peaches smashed into the wall next to me. He fell to the ground, shook off the impact, and growled, entering 'shred and maim' mode.

On the other side of the living room stood a figure. He wore a white cloak, covered in runes, over gray combat armor. Two guns rested in thigh holsters. Blades rested on both forearms, and he stood, arms crossed, with a small smile on his lips as he stared down at Corbel.

"Strong, back off," Corbel said. "I'll deal with this."

"A Lucent?" Monty muttered under his breath. "I thought they had all been captured?"

The Lucent looked at Corbel and then glanced at me. He dismissed me without a second look. I drew Grim Whisper as Peaches padded over to my side with a low rumble.

<I'm going to bite him now.>

I rested a hand on Peaches' head.

<One second, boy. Corbel wants to talk with him. You can bite him later.>

"Where is it?" the Lucent asked, giving Peaches a second glance.

"Where is what?" Corbel stared hard at the Lucent. "What are you talking about?"

"You dare feign ignorance, lapdog? The soulkeeper. Where did your master hide it?"

Corbel's face was a stone mask. "You're making a serious mistake," Corbel answered, looking around. "This is the residence of Hades' wife, Persephone. Who are you looking for?"

"I'm well aware of who lives here," the Lucent answered. "Why not prolong your life? I'll dispatch you last if you hand over the soulkeeper."

"Thank you for the offer, but I have no idea what you're referring to," Corbel replied. "I think you should go—now."

The Lucent narrowed his eyes and glared at Corbel. It was, I have to say, at least a two on the glare-o-meter. I was almost impressed, but I got the feeling he was trying too hard.

"I will find it," the Lucent said with a vicious smile. "When I do, she will be beyond his reach and Hades will be lost."

"What is he talking about?" I asked. "What is this soulkeeper thing? What does he mean, Hades will be lost?"

"Stay out of this, Strong," Corbel answered without looking at me. "You have no idea who or what he is."

"He tried to hurt Peaches," I said, letting the anger flow into my voice. "Get out of my way, Hound."

"You would do well to listen to Hades' lapdog, human," the Lucent said. "That is, if you enjoy living."

I fired Grim Whisper and it punched several entropy rounds into Mr. Condescending, blasting him back across the living room. His body tumbled over one of the chaise lounges and crashed to the floor.

"And *that's* how you deal with a threat," I said, holstering Grim Whisper. "Who *was* that, Corbel?"

"My name is Alnit the First," said a voice from behind the chaise. "Leader of the Lightbringers."

Corbel started backing up. "I told you I'd deal with this," Corbel said through gritted teeth. "Now, this is going to be…difficult."

"Lightbringers," Monty said, "is he referring to the

Lucent?"

"The one and the same," Corbel replied, nodding and opening his coat. "No one calls them Lucent anymore, except mages."

"Bloody hell," Monty said under his breath. "This may be a good time for a strategic retreat."

"Are we talking about running away?" I asked as we started backing up together. "What exactly is he? Just asking, because he shrugged off all my entropy rounds."

"The time for retreat was before we entered the building," Corbel answered. "He's been waiting for us. This was a trap."

"Indeed," Alnit said, standing effortlessly, as if I hadn't just hit him with a magazine of entropy rounds. "I've been tasked with your elimination."

I don't miss.

The alternative was that this Alnit Lightbringer was stronger than my rounds. Anyone or anything that could shrug off entropy rounds deserved serious respect. It was a shame I was fresh out of respect today.

"Okay, Walnut," I said, switching magazines. "I think you're going to find *that* harder than you think."

"Walnut?" Alnit said, narrowing his eyes at me. "Are you mocking me?"

"Strong," Corbel said under his breath, "not all of us have been cursed alive, you know."

"I'm aware," I said, stepping forward. "I'll get his attention."

"You don't *want* his attention," Corbel snapped back. "Shit, Strong, you're going to get us all killed."

"I think that's his plan anyway," I said, unsheathing

Ebonsoul. "Might as well make it difficult."

"I see," Alnit said, focusing on me and drawing one of his forearm blades. "You are different. You've been touched."

"In more ways than one," Monty muttered, forming a white-hot flame orb. "Who sent you?"

"Do not presume to question me, mage," Alnit replied. "I only answer to one."

"Does this *one* have a name?" Monty asked. "Or is he nameless?"

Corbel stared at Monty. "You're both insane!"

"It's a simple question, really," Monty replied. "I'm asking who he answers to."

Alnit gestured with a hand.

A mini-shockwave erupted in the living room, obliterating the furniture and clearing the floor. The energy blast shoved Monty and Corbel back, leaving Peaches and me untouched.

I glanced at Corbel. "Let the record state that Walnut disintegrated the living room," I said, looking at the destruction. "That's almost Monty-level blasting. Impressive."

<Can I bite him now?>

<He seems dangerous. If you can bite him without getting hurt, then yes. If not, stay back.>

<I'm going to bite him, and then, you can get me sausage.>

<Let me try and convince him to leave.>

<With a knife?>

<It's very persuasive.>

<So are my fangs.>

<Stay back for now, and let me talk to him.>

"Where's Persephone?" I asked as Alnit turned to

face me. "Did *you* kidnap her?"

We were standing in the makeshift arena he had created. He shrugged off his cloak and stepped into the center of the living room.

"A wager, then?" Alnit asked as he tossed the blade into the air and caught it hilt first. "Are you game?"

Entropy rounds barely tickled him.

Ebonsoul was no ordinary blade. If I managed to cut him, it would siphon his energy and feed it to me. It was also a seraph, designed to destroy creatures of hell, specifically demons.

I didn't know where Alnit was from, but I expected my having a seraph would add the extra bite I needed to shred him, or so I hoped.

"What kind of wager?" I asked. "I'm not really a gambling man."

"Does he fight for all of you?" Alnit asked, looking past me at Monty and Corbel.

"No," Corbel said quickly, "there's no way he—"

"Yes," Monty said, and absorbed the flame orb. "He does."

"Are you deranged?" Corbel asked, whirling on Monty. "You *know* what a Lucent is. There's no way Simon can win."

"Thanks for the vote of confidence," I said. "Remind me to call you whenever I feel all is lost and there's no hope."

"You have no idea what you're facing, Strong," Corbel said. "This fight is over before it's begun. Even with your curse."

"I've seen him stand against things that should have torn him to shreds," Monty said. "He's too stubborn to lose."

"I don't know who's crazier, Strong for going up against a Lightbringer, or you for trusting him," Corbel said, shaking his head. "We're all dead."

Alnit smiled. "Very well, Cursed One," he said. "If you manage to draw blood before I slay you, I will stay your execution for three of your days."

"Three days? That's generous," I said. "Wouldn't want you to inconvenience yourself."

"Do you agree to the terms?"

"And if I don't?"

"I will slay you, the mage, Hades' lapdog, and the Hellhound," Alnit said, pointing to each of us in turn. "Slowly and painfully."

"I fight together with my Hellhound. Do you have a problem with that?"

Alnit waved my words away. "Your Hellhound is a pup. Are you certain you want to place him in harm's way?"

"He can take care of himself," I said, looking down at the rumbling Peaches. "He's a lot tougher than he looks."

"I certainly hope the same holds true for you as well."

"This wager seems lopsided," I said. "What happens when I defeat you?"

"When you…defeat me?" Alnit laughed for a good ten seconds. Clearly, he was feeling confident in his ability. "*If* you cut me, I will honor my word. If you fall without drawing blood, you and your comrades will perish here by my hand."

I reached in my jacket and pulled out my silver flask

of Valhalla Java. The blue grinning skulls radiated power as I uncapped it. One day, if I survived this little tango, I'd have to ask Ezra what kind of magic created a liquid to match the perfect desire of the drinker.

For me, it held what I considered to be javambrosia—coffee of the gods. I raised the flask to my lips and took a long swig. Warmth flooded my body and I felt the energy course through me. If I was going to face a homicidal maniac—coffee was essential.

"That *is* orlandgasmic," I said, reverently inhaling the aroma wafting up to my nose. "I cut you, and you back off for three days?"

"Correct," Alnit said with a nod. "The alternative is I end your existence now."

Monty stepped close to my side.

"One moment, your lightness," I said, holding up a finger. "Strategy meeting."

"Please, consult your mage," Alnit said with a small smile. "For all the good it will do."

We stepped a few feet away and out of earshot.

"That's not arrogance, is it?" I asked Monty. "He took my entropy rounds like I was firing spitballs."

"The Lucent were thought to be a myth," Monty said, rubbing his chin. "They aren't deities, but the closest equivalent you would understand would be fallen angels."

"Are we talking biblical-level power here? Lucifer and his crew?" I asked. "Because I'm holding a seraph blade here."

"No, I'm not making any kind of biblical reference," Monty said, looking over at Alnit. "And as far as I know, that whole 'being cast out of Heaven' myth is a bit of a stretch."

"I'm not really getting the myth vibe here," I said, glancing over at Alnit. "Angels? Not seeing it. No wings, halo, or harp. Are you serious? Because if that's the case, he looks more like a special-ops angel than one of the choir."

"I said the closest equivalent *you* would understand." Monty placed a hand on my shoulder. "That, however, is irrelevant."

"Oh, I don't know," I said, "considering how much damage Grim Whisper did, I think it's kind of relevant."

"You don't have to defeat him, just cut him before he kills you," Monty replied. "More importantly—we need an exit. In case your initial attempt fails."

I looked past Monty to the door.

"The door?" I asked. "You can just walk out."

Monty shook his head. "Barriers are in place to prevent our exit. Stronger than anything I've felt. We're going to need an alternate exit. If you provide an opening, I can facilitate an egress."

"Are you saying he won't honor the terms of the wager?"

"He's been sent here to *kill* us," Monty replied. "I don't happen to know any honorable assassins. Do you?"

"Good point," I said. "You realize we're thirty floors up?"

"I'm aware," Monty said. "One more thing…"

"More than my imminent death, you mean?"

"The Lucent are *patternists*."

"Let's pretend that word means nothing to me," I

said. "Because unless we're about to have a fabric showdown, I don't know what a patternist is."

"Lucents observe and decipher patterns," Monty said. "You must be unpredictable, or he will read your attacks and neutralize them, and you."

"Wonderful," I said. "How long before he can read my 'pattern'? Do you know?"

"According to the texts, it can range anywhere from twenty-five to thirty seconds," Monty replied, stepping back. "I'd try to end this quickly."

"How do you even know this?" I asked, entering a defensive stance. "This sounds obscure even for mage study."

"It is," Monty said, "but Professor Ziller insisted on having the mages in his classes study what he called the 'uncommon lore,' in addition to regular mythos."

"Ziller and uncommon make perfect sense."

I focused on my breath. I had thirty seconds on the outside to face some kind of angelic-type being, cut him with Ebonsoul, or be crushed.

No pressure.

<Hey, boy. You can sit this one out if you think it's too dangerous.>

<If I bite the bad man, will the angry man make me some of the big sausage?>

<Boy, I don't think you want—>

Peaches blinked out the next second.

SIX

THERE'S SOMETHING TO be said for having a singular focus. I raced at Alnit, knowing Peaches would materialize close to him.

Thirty seconds.

I slid forward and lunged.

Alnit dodged my thrust and stepped to the side with a slash. I parried his attack as my Hellhound appeared next to his leg, fangs first. He continued his rotation and swatted down in an outward arc, sending Peaches flying.

Peaches smashed into and through the bay window. I glanced at Monty as if to say, 'there's your opening.' I wasn't overly worried about Peaches. He'd teleported from worse situations. That didn't mean I appreciated Walnut ejecting my Hellhound from the thirtieth floor of The Eldorado.

<Find someplace safe to stay.>

<I didn't get to bite him.>

<He's too dangerous. Get safe. I'll make sure Monty makes you an extra-large sausage.>

<Promise?>

<Promise. Now, get safe.>

<Don't get flakey. Extra-large sausage.>

<It's don't flake out, and no more talking to the lizard.>

I stepped to the side and slashed upward. Alnit blocked my attack with his blade and a grin.

"Well done," he said, locking blades. "It would seem you have a small amount of skill. Even without your Hellhound."

He was stronger than I imagined. I barely held on to Ebonsoul as Alnit pushed against me.

"Just enough to make a difference," I said, shifting my bodyweight. "Wouldn't want you to get bored."

I kicked out and connected solidly with his knee. Kicking marble would've felt softer. His leg didn't budge. Alnit twisted his body with a quick reversal. A fist buried itself in my ribs and launched me back across the bloodwood floor. I smashed into the wall in a heap of pain, with ample doses of agony every time I inhaled.

I got to my feet through the haze of pain as my body flushed hot, knitting the bones Alnit had just cracked. Being immortal didn't mean I was immune to pain. It just meant that I didn't die and stay dead. I felt pain, and it was never a picnic.

"You should be writhing in agony," Alnit said. "Yet, you still stand. Excellent."

"Sorry to disappoint," I said through clenched teeth. "I'm going to save all my writhing for later, if that's okay with you."

He stepped forward and disappeared, moving faster than my eyes could track. I ducked reflexively and felt the displacement of air as his blade slashed over my head.

A knee crashed into my chest as he slashed downward. I raised Ebonsoul in an upper block, pivoted my body, and cut upward. The runes in my blade flared red as it bit into his skin, drawing blood.

Alnit saw the blood and smiled. That's when I knew.

He had never planned to let us leave this place alive.

SEVEN

EBONSOUL SIPHONED ENERGY and slammed my body with power. Together with the javambrosia from the flask, a surge of power rushed through me.

Alnit raised an eyebrow as I shoved him back.

"What are you?" he asked, looking at the blood dripping down his arm. "Where did you get that weapon?"

"I'm the one who cut you," I said. "I get the feeling the whole 'three days' thing was just smoke. Right?"

Alnit nodded with a short laugh. "Astute for a human," he said. "I merely shared what I thought you'd like to hear."

"Monty?" I asked. "Are you ready?"

"I need ten more seconds," Monty replied, his voice tight. "I'm reconfiguring the runes. Can you keep him busy?"

"Wait," Corbel said, "reconfiguring the runes? What does that mean?"

"I'm sure I can keep the Lightbulb here busy," I said, dodging a slash and back-stepping from a fist aimed at my head. "But I think he's getting upset."

I drew Grim Whisper, rotated around another thrust, and placed the barrel of my gun in Alnit's face, firing. Every round punched his head, making him stumble back from the impact with little effect. He slid back across the living room floor, temporarily blinded by the black energy clinging to his face.

I saw the runes in the floor begin to glow and then pulse with golden light. The golden light traveled along the floor and crept up the walls.

"I doubt that's a good sign," I muttered under my breath. "I thought you couldn't read the protozoa runes?"

"Proto-runes are the ones outside in the hallway," Monty replied, making his way to the window. "These are just old."

"Tristan?" Corbel asked, concern lacing his voice. "What the hell are you doing?"

"I'm wondering the same thing, Monty," I said. "Walnut over there just stepped past upset and into full-blown pissed."

"Taking the Hellhound exit," Monty said, leaping up to the windowsill and peering out over the edge. "The runic configuration blocked any teleportation circles. We'll have to clear their influence before I can relocate us. You have ten seconds until the release."

Monty disappeared from sight, as a stunned Corbel stared at me. "He's crazier than you are," he said slowly. "Did he really just—?"

"Finally," I said with a sigh of relief. "You see? I'm the *sane* one."

"Hellhound exit?" Corbel asked, looking around with

a confused expression. "Ten seconds until the release of what?"

"Stupid human, your pathetic weapon will not help you," Alnit said, ripping off the last of the black energy from his face. "I will crush you and your—?"

Alnit looked around.

"Raincheck on the crushing," I said, and leaped up to the sill. "Corbel—this is the designated Hellhound exit. Take it or stay and play with your friend, Walnut the Light."

"Monty," I said, pressing the main bead of my mala bracelet, causing my shield to materialize in front of my body, "I so hate you right now."

I stepped out of The Eldorado, and into space.

EIGHT

I SPREAD OUT my arms.

The shield acted like a wing and slowed my descent somewhat, but not by much. I looked up once I heard the screaming. For a second, I thought it was Walnut the Lightsaber, but he was still in The Eldorado, looking out of the window, observing our imminent flattening with a malicious smile.

Above me and to my right, I saw the body of a flailing and screaming Corbel. The grimace of fear and anger on his face made me feel warm all over.

I couldn't help but smile.

The human body reached terminal velocity around fifty-three meters a second. Considering that I jumped from the thirtieth floor of The Eldorado, and factoring in air friction, it meant I had about four-and-a-half seconds before I became one with the sidewalk.

Four-and-a-half seconds was a lifetime.

An energy spike shifted above us with a bass *thwump,* as a blinding golden light filled the sky like a second sun. Most of the wall near the window collapsed in on itself, disappearing from view.

"Your bloody mage just killed us," Corbel yelled at me, as a green teleportation circle rushed up, winking him out of existence with a bright flash.

I turned in time to see another green circle race at me with a blinding flash. When I could see again, my shield was gone, and I was surrounded by grass, lying on my back.

A wet rag slapped my cheek, drenching my face. I looked up and caught a faceful of Hellhound saliva and sausage breath. Old sausage breath.

<Stop breathing on me, ugh.>

I tried to shove my Hellhound away, and succeeded in sliding backward on the grass. He looked down at me and shook his massive head, dousing me with more projectile slobber.

<You should eat more meat. You will be stronger.>

<I'm strong enough. Thank you. If you ate less, you'd be easier to move.>

<Do you feel better now?>

<I was fine until you tried to drown me in your saliva.>

<My saliva just saved you. I think that deserves a sausage.>

<You don't, and your slobber of epic proportions didn't. Now, move back. I can't see where we are.>

"Intact," I heard Corbel say, his voice angry. "I said...*intact*."

We were in the center of a clearing, a few hundred feet away from the Tarr-Coyne Wild West Playground and several blocks away from The Eldorado.

The sound of sirens filled the air as I slid to one side and looked over the trees to The Eldorado. One of the towers was a smoking, blasted husk. My phone vibrated in my pocket. I looked down at the number, pinched the bridge of my nose, and grimaced.

It was Ramirez, the NYTF Director. Shit.

The New York Task Force, or NYTF, was a quasi-military police force, created to deal with any supernatural event occurring in New York City. They were paid to deal with the things that couldn't be explained to the general public without causing mass hysteria.

They were led by Angel Ramirez, who was one of the best directors the NYTF had ever had. He currently wanted to rip me into several small pieces, and then probably set those pieces on fire, while using hydrochloric acid to douse the flames.

I took a deep breath and prepared for the inevitable meltdown. As soon as he'd heard we were near The Eldorado, he'd read me the riot act.

"Hey, Angel. What's going—?" I began before he cut me off.

"No," Ramirez answered, his voice clipped. "Don't 'Hey, Angel' me. I have so many agencies on my ass, it feels like a bureaucratic colonoscopy."

"Ouch, sounds invasive," I answered. "What did you do?"

"What did I do?" He took a deep breath. "What did *I* do?"

"Strong, tell me you aren't near The Eldorado," Ramirez said, his voice calm with an undercurrent of fury. "Tell me that nightmare you call a vehicle isn't parked in front of said building, scaring the hell out of the first responders and impeding my men from doing their job."

"Well, we—" I started.

"Tell me," Ramirez said, his voice going up in volume, "that you had nothing to do with the explosion that just blasted the South Tower of a landmark building owned by one of the most influential companies in this city."

"We were following a lead and—" I tried again.

"Get your cursed car out of my scene and—"

A string of bilingual curses followed. Ramirez was fast approaching bleeding ear levels. He was loud enough that I could hold the phone at arm's length and still hear him clearly. After a few seconds, he took a breath. I quickly put the phone back to my ear.

"On it," I said before extending my arm again.

"Now!" he screamed and hung up.

I stood slowly and waited for the earth to stop seesawing before heading over to where Monty and Corbel stood. Judging from his tone, the Hound of Hades was having a bad day.

"You let that maniac face off against a Lucent, knowing he couldn't defeat it!" Corbel yelled over the sirens of the emergency personnel vehicles racing to the site of The Eldorado. "What the hell were you thinking?"

"Simon," Monty said, nodding in my direction, "was the only one who could have stood against Alnit, and bought us the time needed to find an exit."

"An exit?" Corbel asked incredulously. "You call what we just did—*an exit*?"

"We *are* outside the building," I said. "Technically, it's an—"

"Don't," Corbel said, raising a finger without looking

in my direction. "Just don't."

"It's just a bit of structural damage," I said. "Hades is a god, it's—"

"Of the *Underworld*," Corbel shot back. "Not New York City. Do you honestly think he goes around advertising he's a *god*?"

I rubbed my chin in thought. "That would be a problem. No one would believe him anyway. Not without lots of special effects—some dark fog, maybe a few skulls, and wailing from souls and such."

Corbel stared at me with a look of disgust. At least I thought it was disgust. It was possible he needed to use the bathroom. I wouldn't have blamed him. Teleportation circles wreaked havoc with my digestive system.

"There was no way we could have defeated the leader of the Lightbringers," Monty replied, heading out of the park. "Not without several mages."

"But you let *Strong* face him?"

"Simon's job wasn't to *defeat* Alnit," Monty explained. "He was meant to *distract* him."

"I probably could've taken him," I said, cracking my neck as we headed to Central Park West. "I was holding back."

"You shot him point blank in the face with entropy rounds," Corbel answered. "All it did was obscure his vision for a few seconds."

"Like I said," I answered, "I was holding back."

"You're both insane," Corbel muttered as we left the park. "Hades is mad to trust you two."

I looked ahead and realized Central Park West, south of 91st Street, was closed off and barricaded for several blocks in both directions. Fire trucks, regular ambulances, NYTF squad cars, and a group of the blue EMTe vehicles filled the street and sidewalks.

Sitting in the middle of the block between 91st and 90th streets was the Dark Goat.

The cars in front of and behind it had been crushed into abstract art. The Dark Goat sat unscathed. Flatbed tow trucks had been brought in to remove the debris, but no one approached the Dark Goat.

"Why didn't you use the circles inside the apartment?" I asked, smiling at the wide berth everyone gave the Dark Goat.

"The runes inside Persephone's home hindered my ability to cast the circles," Monty replied. "Once we were out of range, I was able to utilize them."

"Not that I didn't enjoy the trip, but can we avoid making that a regular thing?" I asked. "Freefall teleportation is not as fun as it sounds."

"Duly noted." Monty glanced over at me. "You're not suffering any ill effects from the circle?"

"If you mean does my stomach want to claw out of my body?" I asked. "No. A little queasy, but nothing extreme."

"I wonder if it has something to do with the elixir in your flask," Monty answered. "I'd like to run some tests on it when we have time."

"Sure," I said. "Did Dex teach you the flying teleportation circles? Or is this part of what's happening with your shift?"

Monty shook his head.

"I've been reviewing Ziller's treatise on quantum spatial mechanics," Monty said. "I'm nowhere near the expertise level of my uncle, but the execution is fairly straightforward. An unfixed teleportation circle is, in essence, a mobile trans-dimensional tunnel."

"Like a magical wormhole?"

Monty cocked his head to one side and glanced at me.

"You've been paying attention," he said. "That's a simplistic definition, but not entirely inaccurate."

"So when Han punches it and jumps into hyperspace —?"

"No," Monty said, cutting me off. "Hyperspace is not a trans-dimensional tunnel. That is a fictional construct set in space."

I nodded. "Right, trans-dimensional tunnel is magic-based," I said, not understanding a word after 'Ziller' but realizing it was nearly impossible to stop Monty in the middle of his magespeak explanations. "Not sci-fi and, therefore, impossible."

"Precisely," he continued. "I did have to compensate for the velocity and displace the accumulated energy of the fall. My rough calculations had you hitting the sidewalk at over two hundred thousand joules. This is why we landed several blocks way."

"What about the Bajoran wormhole?" I asked. "That one was stable."

"And also a fictional construct," Monty said with a sigh. "The closest science has come to explaining it is the Einstein-Rosen bridge. Maybe you've heard of it?"

"When did they name a bridge after Einstein?" I asked. "Not that he doesn't deserve it."

Monty gave me a 'you can't be serious' look and kept on explaining about his trans-dimensional tunnels. I tuned out most of it, my brain processing the events unfolding around us. I didn't even try to wrap my brain around his explanation. I was just glad I hadn't had to test my immortality against a city sidewalk.

"That's why I was able to use the mobile teleportation circles," Monty finished with a look of satisfaction. "You really should read up on Ziller. His quantum theory of runic displacement is fascinating."

"The next time I can't sleep, I'll be sure to dive in, Mr. Spock."

"Simon, you're using magic."

"You didn't hear about the deathane?"

"In great detail, yes," he replied. "I understand it was an olfactory nightmare."

"Then you understand why it's safer if I don't try and use magic, or energy, or chakras, or whatever it's called."

"Granted, you've had limited success, but you can get better. You only need to practice."

"You knew I couldn't beat the Walnut," I said, keeping my voice low. Monty glanced back at Corbel. "Right?"

"It was a calculated risk," Monty replied. "If the Lucent are involved, we'll need more information. This is going to get worse—much worse. The Lucent were relegated to Tartarus."

"Tartar sauce?"

He gave me a 'don't try my patience' stare before answering. I had a few more tartar-related comments I immediately filed for future use.

"*Tartarus* is an abyssal prison located beneath the Underworld," Monty replied. "It's rumored to hold the Titans."

"And the Lucent come from there?"

"The Lucent serve there."

"Serve there?" I asked. "Who do they serve there?"

"Tartarus," Monty said, his voice grim. "If he's involved with Persephone's disappearance, I doubt Hades can remain uninvolved."

"What is it with giving the place and the deity the same name?" I asked. "Don't they realize how confusing that can be?"

"If Tartarus is involved, perhaps you can convince an eons old entity to change his name—possibly to something easier…like Steve?"

"How powerful is this Tartarsauce person?"

"Originally, he's considered a primordial force or deity."

"Why am I not liking the sound of that?" I said. "The last time we faced a primordial anything, it was —"

"Chaos."

"Shit," I said. "Do we know anyone who can face this Tartar guy?"

"I'd have to say we are grossly underqualified to face this foe," Monty replied with a sigh. "I think even the Olympians would have trouble in this scenario. We are certainly outmatched in power."

"When has that ever stopped us?" I asked. "Maybe we can get Hades to actually participate this time? I mean, Persephone is *his* wife."

"That is precisely why he *can't* act," Monty answered. "If he takes action and Tartarus is involved, Persephone's life may be at risk."

"Are we sure Tartarboy has Persephone?" I asked.

"Maybe she just ran away?"

"Simon..." Monty said, his voice more serious than usual. This was a feat, since Monty only had a few settings: serious, grave, somber, and grim. "Do not prod Hades. This situation must be highly upsetting and he's likely to blast you for being, well...you."

I raised my hands in surrender. "No prodding from me," I said. "But I will have to ask him some questions if he wants us to find her."

We approached the blue EMTe ambulances parked around the entrance of The Eldorado.

"EMTe" stood for EMT elite. The NYTF used these paramedics whenever they encountered some kind of supernatural disaster, or when Monty was allowed to run rampant, which was pretty much the same thing. The medics all wore dark red uniforms and drove around in extra-large, blue, rune-covered ambulances.

They were the Navy Seals of the paramedics. Tough as two-day-old steak and willing to risk their lives no matter the situation. Some of them had magical healing ability, and they all possessed certain 'sensitivity' to supernatural phenomena. "It would seem your presence in the city is keeping the EMTe busy again," Corbel said behind us. "They must have been bored out of their minds when you two were away."

We had been out of the city, in London, for a short time a while back. After that, we had tried to keep the devastation to the city to a minimum.

If you overlooked the destruction of Peck Slip, which was really Kraggy's fault, or the reconstruction of Gracie Mansion—all Monty, I'd say we were doing a pretty good job of low-key demolition. Until today, when Monty decided to reconfigure the protozoic runes in Mrs. Hades' place.

A few of the faces were familiar as I looked around. I noticed the EMTe medics weren't treating anyone, and I took that as a good sign. I wasn't among the injured for once. It was a welcome change, not being scrutinized or used as part of the rookie hazing.

I had become a widely discussed topic among the EMTe community, given my peculiar 'condition.' Most of them took it in stride, giving me space and time to let my body heal itself. Others, the rookies, always tried to help me, only to be shocked when I recuperated before their eyes from something that should have killed me.

The veterans were used to me by now, and they nodded in my direction when I walked past.

"Well, well, look who it is. The team responsible for renovating the city. One building at a time."

I recognized the voice and cringed.

Frank.

"I believe this one is yours," Monty said without turning around.

"Are you two actively targeting structures in this city?" Frank asked, his gravelly voice rasping behind us. "You realize this building is a landmark?"

Frank defined grizzled: older, mid-sixties, built like a wall and probably as tough. He was the oldest EMTe still in the field and was affectionately known as the OG. I thought it meant "old gangsta," but one of the other EMTe told me it meant "original geezer."

"Hey, Frank," I said, turning to face him. "When are you going to retire?"

"The same day you and your friends stop breaking my city," he answered around an unlit cigar. "Heard we had jumpers—who happened to vanish on their way to the sidewalk. Know anything about that?"

"We just got here," I lied. "Don't know about any jumpers."

"Right," Frank answered, squinting past me and pointing with his cigar. "That's not your indestructomobile parked over there next to the impressionist art that used to be parked cars?"

"*That's* where I left it," I said, looking at the unscathed Dark Goat. "We were just taking a walk in the park when I heard the explosion."

Frank looked down at Peaches and shook his head slowly.

"Stop jerking my chain," he said, chewing on the cigar again. "I'd know if you were walking around in the park with that beast you call a dog. I'd hear the screams from across town."

Corbel stepped around us and headed into The Eldorado. I looked at Monty, who nodded and followed him.

"Listen, Frank," I said, lowering my voice, "we're working a case and—"

Frank held up a hand. "Don't want to know," he said. "Lucky for you, all of the damage was contained to the structure. The Landmark Commission is going to chew your agency a new one for this, though."

"This wasn't us."

Frank nodded sagely. "Of course not," he replied. "Just like Gracie Mansion, or Peck Slip, or any of the other renovation and restoration projects you two cause. I'm actually surprised London is still intact."

"We left London in one piece, mostly," I said, trying to change the subject. "We were only there a short time. Wait, how do you know about London?"

Frank gave me a mischievous smile.

"I'm old, not stupid, Strong," he replied. "EMTe is connected—*worldwide.* Anywhere you and your friend go, you tend to leave a depression."

"You mean impression?"

"I said what I meant," he growled. "Why don't you and your agency take another vacation? To Antarctica?"

I thought back to our trip to London. Most of the damage there was a result of Thomas and his twisted plan.

"It wasn't a vacation," I said. "Anyway, London suffered minimal damage."

"Minimal damage?" Frank said, nearly choking on his cigar. "I'd hate to see maximum. I think they're still rebuilding the Tate."

"*That* monstrosity of a building needed a makeover," I said, heading to the entrance of The Eldorado. Peaches padded silently next to me. "I need to go upstairs. Can you make sure no one goes near the car?"

"Like anyone wants to get near that thing," Frank answered with a shudder. "Makes my skin crawl just looking at it."

"I'm serious. It's dangerous."

"I know," Frank answered. "You and it better be gone before Ramirez gets here."

"Working on it," I said before I entered the building.

NINE

THE LOBBY WAS a hive of activity.

NYTF had control of the scene and let me through with little trouble. Most of that was due to the Peaches Effect. Anytime I needed to clear an area, I'd just let my Hellhound walk a little ahead of me. Those who didn't know me cleared the way for Peaches.

I saw Monty and Corbel standing near the elevator banks.

"We're going back up there because…?"

I looked at the elevator and realized it was being stopped several floors before the penthouse.

"Because, aside from being monumentally pissed," Corbel started, "Hades is going to want to know the extent of the damage. For insurance purposes."

"Who would insure the god of the Underworld?" I asked as we stepped onto the elevator. More creaking as Peaches stepped on. "Nevermind, I don't think I want to know."

"You may want to feed him something other than slabs of beef," Corbel said, looking down at Peaches.

"He's packing on the pounds."

"I'm going to put him on an exercise program."

Corbel shook his head. "You can't put a Hellhound on an exercise program," he answered, shaking his head some more. "You need to get him training. He's not a *dog,* you know."

"Really? I wasn't aware. What gave it away? The omega beams? Or growing to the size of a small bus in battlemode?"

"Mori is good, but you need someone else," Corbel said, patting Peaches on the head and managing to keep his hand. "He needs real training."

"The last time I tried that," I said, remembering Peaches' last and only training session, "it didn't go so well."

"I heard," Corbel answered. "Give me a call once we deal with this Persephone situation. I'll put you in touch with another trainer."

"I seriously doubt you know someone better than Ezra or Mori," I answered, "but we can discuss that later. Right now, you're doing an insurance assessment. So, is this where you say 'Fifteen minutes could save Hades fifteen percent or more'?"

"I really hope Alnit is upstairs waiting for you," Corbel said. "Maybe he could silence that fantastic wit of yours."

"I doubt he's up there," I said, looking at Monty. "He's *not* up there, is he?"

"It's unlikely," Monty rubbed his chin. "The runes were reconfigured to exhibit entropic properties."

"Entropic properties?" I asked. "Is that why the tower isn't spread out all over Central Park?"

Monty nodded. "That, and the activation I set off was contained to a small part of the residence. If all of the runes in the penthouse were triggered, most of the building would be gone."

"My entropy rounds only got him angry."

"The runes in the apartment are significantly stronger than your rounds," Monty answered, looking up when we stopped on the twenty-eighth floor. "It would seem this is as far as we can go."

We stepped out on the twenty-eighth floor and took the stairs up. NYTF personnel were scattered all around the two floors. A few kept guard on the stairwell, moving to the side when Peaches came through.

"How does it help Hades to know the extent of the damages?" I asked, trying to figure out why Corbel would want to come back up here. There was something he wasn't sharing.

It's not that I was scared. I was exhibiting a healthy aversion to a creature that could take entropy rounds to the face and only be mildly inconvenienced.

"There may be something that can help us locate Persephone," Corbel replied.

"Hades, the CEO, wants to know how bad the damage is, and you're going to tell him what? We blew up the tower, and the Lucent left?"

"*We*," Corbel said, climbing the stairs, "did no such thing. You, Tristan, and your renegade Hellhound did the destroying. I was trying to de-escalate the situation."

"Alnit was there to kill us. What were you de-escalating it to—a maiming?"

"Some of the pieces in this residence are priceless," Corbel answered, ignoring my question. "If they're gone—"

"Maybe I'm not seeing it," I started, "but wouldn't Hades be more concerned that his wife is missing than with the destruction of any of the pieces in the residence?"

"Of course," Corbel added quickly. "It's just that he's not used to being attacked. It's not going well, and now, this."

"He should have known there was a risk when he asked for us," I said. "We aren't exactly the delicate solution."

"I'm sure he's aware of your methods," Corbel answered, opening the door to the thirtieth floor. "Everyone in the city is aware of your methods."

"Our reputation precedes us," I said. "That's what happens when you do good work."

"Good work." Corbel shook his head. "You keep telling yourself that."

We stepped into the hallway that led to the triplex. None of the runes were active, which meant the hallway was dormant. Corbel opened the door to Persephone's place.

He stood there transfixed for several seconds, shook his head, and glanced at me.

"This will *not* go well," Corbel said under his breath. "I hope, for your sake, that you're really immortal, Strong."

I stepped to the door and looked past Corbel. Everything was fine until you looked beyond the entrance. One of the staircases was missing, along with the entire living room, and part of the upper level of the triplex.

"In what reality is this *my* fault?" I asked, annoyed. "Was I the one who reconfigured the runes? No. Am I the next level kick-ass mage? No. Do I work for a god? No. Is my title the Hound of anything?"

"No. However, you *are* the one bonded to a hound capable of indescribable amounts of destruction," Monty answered, with the hint of a smile.

"Are you implying guilt by association?" I snapped. "That somehow, by just knowing you and Peaches, I had something to do with this and any of the destruction you both cause?"

Monty raised a finger.

"In addition to being in proximity to every instance of demolition perpetrated by the Montague & Strong Detective Agency. In fact, one could say, you're the common thread, the essence of commonality, which ties all of the destruction together."

"What he said," Corbel added. "Every time something gets destroyed, you aren't far away."

"You know what I've realized?" I asked, containing the anger. "After all the destruction we've caused, and when I say *we,* I mean *you* and my trusty Hellhound?"

"Do tell," Monty said. "Please, enlighten me."

"You can't spell damage without '*mage*'."

"Astute, but ultimately irrelevant," Monty replied. "The fact is, you are a destruction magnet."

I stood there at a loss for words.

"You know what?" I said after a few seconds. "Both of you need to go to—"

Another explosion rocked the tower, cutting me off.

TEN

"THAT. WASN'T. ME."

"I know," Monty answered, looking out into the damaged area. "We're running out of time."

Monty released a burst of energy and formed a large green circle on the floor around us. He closed his eyes for a second, orienting himself with his back facing the gaping hole that used to be the living room.

"What did you do?" I asked, looking at Monty, who was gesturing. "Was that a delayed rune?"

"*That* was the sonic equivalent of impending doom," Monty answered, gesturing even faster. "Corbel, if you need to retrieve an item, I suggest haste."

Corbel ran into the triplex, which was probably closer to a duplex now. I closed my eyes and let my senses expand. A wave of angry energy washed over me, stealing my breath.

"Shit," I said with a gasp. "We need to go. Now."

Peaches rumbled and whined next to me. He stepped into a 'defend and maim' stance, turning to face the former living room.

<*Something bad is coming.*>

<*Monty is working on a portal. Get ready to jump in.*>

"Corbel!" I yelled. "We're leaving, with or without you—now."

"I need a moment!" he yelled back, and I felt another shift of energy above us. "Got it!"

Corbel leaped off what used to be stairs and landed next to us in a roll. I looked out of the hole that used to be the living room. The energy was approaching faster now. I felt my resolve weaken. All I wanted to do was lie down in a fetal position and wrap my arms around my body.

I stumbled back, with thoughts of surrender and despair clouding my mind. A hard slap rocked my head away from the gap, bringing me clarity.

"What the hell was that?" I asked, shaking the effects off. "All I wanted to do was—"

"Look away or you're finished," Corbel said, grabbing my arm and turning me away from the gap. "Tristan, this would be a good time for that portal."

"Take the center one each time, or you will be lost," Monty said, as white runes flowed from his fingers, forming a portal. "Remember the center—each time."

<*Stay close to me. I don't want you getting lost.*>

<*I never get lost.*>

<*Center portal each time.*>

Monty stepped into the portal and vanished. Corbel shoved me forward and jumped in behind me.

The world went white and hazy.

I sensed Peaches next to me for a few seconds, and then he was gone. Three identical portals opened in front of me. Behind me, I sensed the dark energy getting closer.

I jumped into the second portal, and saw Peaches next to me again. This time, three identical portals formed, stacked one on top of the other. I leaped into the center and found myself in front of three more portals below me. Once again, I chose the center.

The sensation of being chased vanished, and I landed on a hard floor. A few seconds later, my back was nearly shattered as my Hellhound landed on me. I grunted in pain as he padded off, about as delicately as a dump truck, crushing my spine in the process.

"What the hell was that, Monty?" I groaned as I got to my feet. My back screamed at me as warmth flushed my body. "Why all the portals?"

"A syzygy," Monty said, looking at Corbel. "I think it's time we see Hades."

"A what?" I asked, confused. "What's a zigzagy?"

"It means Alnit is still alive and nearly killed us," Monty replied. "He survived the blast. Which is actually quite impressive and concerning at the same time."

"That feeling was Alnit trying to suck the life out of me?"

"Alnit, and at least two others," Corbel said, rubbing his face. "Three Lucents…gods."

"Three Lucents? You mean two more like Alnit are after us?"

"If they were after us, we'd be dead," Corbel answered. "The syzygy was a trigger, almost an afterthought. We left before they could be alerted."

"I think you two just like saying this word—zigziggy."

"A syzygy is created when three bodies arrange in a

straight-line configuration," Monty explained. "It usually refers to celestial bodies. In this context, that sensation you felt was a result of a runic syzygy. I've never experienced one this close."

"What would have happened if it caught us?"

"Nothing pretty," Corbel said. "First, you lose your will to fight, and then, you lose your will to live. Then the Lucents come and grant your wish, and you thank them for it. It's a devastating battlefield weapon and nearly impossible to combat. Tristan, how did you do it?"

"Mobius cast," Monty said. "Each time you chose the center portal, it flipped the vector."

Corbel nodded. "Removing the straight-line configuration, clever."

I looked around. We were standing on a deserted subway platform. Graffiti covered the walls; broken glass and trash littered the ground around us. Along one wall, a staircase led up to nowhere.

Rats the size of small cats skittered across the tracks near us. They gave Peaches a wide berth, some part of their primitive brain aware that getting close to a Hellhound was a bad idea.

"Where are we?" I asked, trying to orient myself. This had to be one of the many abandoned ghost stations that formed part of the NYC subway. I thought I was familiar with them all, but this one was new to me.

"This is the abandoned 91st Street station near Broadway," Monty said, walking down the platform. "It was the best and closest way to break the configuration. The syzygy would be rendered ineffective underground."

"We need to get to Hades," Corbel said, his voice tight. "I need to inform him of this development."

"What did you go back to get?" I asked. "What was so important we nearly got jiggy with it?"

"What?" Corbel answered defensively. "I told you I needed to assess the damage."

"The zigzagy thing was waiting for us," I said, letting the anger creep into my voice. "They knew someone was going back. It was another trap. One that almost ended me. What was it?"

"When we get to Hades, he'll tell you," Corbel answered. "Until then, I can't say."

ELEVEN

I DROVE THE Dark Goat downtown in silence.

Corbel was hiding something, which meant Hades was hiding something and playing with our lives. Typical god move. Everyone was expendable and a pawn in their stupid games.

I pulled up across the street and looked at the building that used to be One New York Plaza. My last memory of the property was thinking that Hades had been rendered into little god bits from an explosion that took out the top of the building—specifically the offices of Terra Sur Global.

Someone had managed to destroy the top half of the building in an attempt to eliminate the god of the Underworld. Hades didn't explode so easily and he'd stepped into the shadows until he could act.

Now, someone had taken his wife, and this smelled like a ploy to get him to show his hand. After that initial attack, Hades had hinted at a deeper game going on. Something was telling me that Persephone wasn't the real target here.

I parked the Dark Goat and activated the anti-theft measures, placing my hand on the surface and locking it with a series of clangs. A wave of orange energy flowed over its surface, ensuring it was properly safeguarded against nuclear attack.

"Cecil is never going to find a way to destroy that Beast," I said as we crossed the street, dodging traffic New York style, which consisted of ignoring all traffic signals. "I'm sure the Dark Goat got hit at The Eldorado, but I didn't see any damage. Not even a scratch."

"The runes Cecil used on that vehicle are similar in construction to some of the symbols I saw at the penthouse," Monty said, looking at the Dark Goat. "However, I do think you may be correct. It may be indestructible."

"It's possible Hades can give him a hand with the Beast," I said, glancing back at the Dark Goat. "Maybe he knows how to undo the runes?"

"Unlikely," Monty said, "but worth a question in any case. Perhaps he's amenable to meeting with Cecil."

We climbed the stairs and walked across the small plaza.

One New York Plaza had undergone extensive changes since our last visit. Even though the address was still technically the same, the building had been given a complete makeover. We were now standing in the newly named Terra Sur Plaza.

I saw the huge Terra Sur logo attached to the north wall of the building and facing uptown. A stylized T intersected an S in a gothic font, with the bottom of the T ending in a drill bit. In the center, where the letters met, was a large glass diamond, illuminated from within.

"What did Hades do?" I asked with a chuckle, looking up at the logo. "Buy the entire building?"

"Yes," Corbel said, nodding at the six women standing outside of the building. "He actually bought the entire city block."

The women were evenly spaced in front of the building. Each one stood in front of a massive column. They all wore identical gunmetal-colored long coats.

Underneath the coats, I noticed the black combat armor. The expressions on their faces were a combination of 'stay back' and 'approach and die.'

I decided to stay back and keep my limbs attached.

"Are they all—?"

"Valkyrie?" Corbel answered, giving the women a sidelong glance as we entered the building. "Yes, I'd stay back if I were you. I think some of them remember you from your last visit."

"Me?" I said as we entered. "I mean, yes, I know I make quite an impression. Few people who meet me can forget being around me. They must remember my incredible charm, the certain *je ne sais quoi* that makes me unforgettable."

"Unforgettable is accurate," Corbel replied. "Though I'm sure anyone who has met you wishes they could."

"Sad to see such envy," I said with a smile. "I'll ask Hades if he'll let you hang out with us more. Expose you to the suaveness that is the Montague & Strong Detective Agency."

"No, thanks," Corbel answered with a shake of his head. "I'd like to limit my exposure to toxic environments."

We entered the lobby and were stopped by security next to the massive wooden reception desk.

The desk was designed to make you feel puny, and it did its job effectively. Corbel went ahead of us and placed his credentials on the desk, pressing a thumb into the surface next to a computer screen.

Monty narrowed his eyes as he scanned the lobby.

"The strongest energy signatures are concentrated on the ground and top floors," Monty said under his breath. "The other signatures are faint and scattered throughout the structure."

"Work crews?" I asked. "Hades may be having them reinforce the defenses. Getting blown up has a way of making a person paranoid."

"I can't tell." Monty scanned again. "The runic interference is stronger this time. These runes are similar to the ones at The Eldorado."

"Photovoltaic?"

Monty just stared at me. "I honestly wonder if you do that intentionally," he said, sighing. "I need some tea."

"Do what intentionally?" I asked with a smile.

Monty waved away my words. "In any case, it would seem the building is sparsely occupied."

"That's a lot of office space to keep unoccupied," I said. "It's only paranoia if they aren't trying to blow you up."

"Keeping the building almost empty isn't exactly blending in for a god. It would call undue attention to the property."

"They're with me," Corbel said, pointing back at us.

"Is he upstairs?"

The woman behind the redwood posing as a desk looked at us over her glasses as she made a call. After a few seconds, she gave us a nod.

"They will still need to be scanned," she said, her clear voice carrying across the lobby. "No exceptions."

She pointed to a smaller desk and followed us with her sky-blue eyes. It was clear that all of the personnel were comprised of Valkyrie.

"Did Hades make another deal with Odin?" I asked as we headed over to the smaller desk. "I'm noticing more Valkyrie than last time."

"The additional security was considered prudent," Corbel answered. "As a deterrent."

"A deterrent? Are you saying the god of the Underworld is in *danger*?"

"I'm saying," Corbel said, lowering his voice as we stepped up to the smaller desk, "that you shouldn't give the on-edge Valkyries a reason to stab you—not that they need much of one."

"Stabby Valkyrie? Maybe less mead or whatever they drink in Valhalla, and more coffee?"

I reflexively checked my jacket for my flask of javambrosia. I had a feeling I was going to need it, if only to offset the effects of teleportation.

Behind the desk stood another woman wearing a white suit. She narrowed her eyes at me. Her bald head threw me for a second, reminding me of Quan.

Spaced out around her, stood five more Valkyrie standing with drawn blades sharp enough to cut you if you glanced at them the wrong way. I noticed the bald woman didn't carry any weapons. I let my senses expand and realized why. She was a mage, and she was stronger than Monty.

Her energy signature felt familiar somehow, but I couldn't place it. She smiled as I looked at her and produced a white orb of whirling energy in one hand.

That's when it rushed back.

"Syght?" I asked, hoping I wasn't making a catastrophic mistake. "If you're here, who's guarding the third gate?"

"Rest assured, the third gate is adequately secured," Syght said. "It's good to *see* you again, Simon."

"Ah," I said, pointing at her with a smile. "I *saw* what you did there."

She nodded and returned the smile.

On occasion, when Erik, the mage running the Hellfire Club, felt like being a pain in the ass, he'd have potential visitors travel through the three gates to gain entry to the Club.

Each gate corresponded to one of the three areas. The first, being body, scanned for any malignant spells, casting or weapons. The second, mind, tested knowledge and its correct transmission. The third and hardest gate, was spirit. It was guarded by five mages, revealing principles and ideals. The five mages represented the five senses. Syght was one of the mages who guarded the third gate.

In order to pass the third gate, a question would be asked. The answer given needed to provide the sixth or elevated sense required to pass the gate.

"You…are a sight for sore—" I started before an elbow from Corbel stopped me. "It's good to see you too."

"You really have no 'off' switch," Corbel muttered. "She's a respected mage on loan to us from the Dark Council. Can you at least pretend to act like an adult?"

"I need to scan all of you," Syght said, with a cough to hide her laugh. "If you would be so kind as to step over here."

She pointed over to an area near the desk. I noticed the large circle on the floor filled with runes.

"Maybe I'm seeing things, but that looks like an—"

"Oblivion circle, yes," Syght finished. "It's currently dormant. If you aren't who you appear to be, it won't remain that way."

I hesitated. Oblivion circles, dormant or not, made me uncomfortable. Something about stepping into a circle that could reduce you to ash seemed unwise.

"Can't you just ask me a question instead?" I asked, keeping to the edge of the circle. "I'm not a big fan of 'oblivion' anything."

"This is merely a formality," Syght said, narrowing her eyes at me. "I see you have established a strong bond with your Hellhound. There is, however, an alternative to the circle."

"I'll take alternative to the circle of death for two hundred, Alex," I said quickly. "What do I have to do?"

"Not much," Syght said with a shrug, "You just have to fight the security personnel around the circle—to the death."

I looked around at the five Valkyrie. All of them nodded and smiled at me. I may be immortal, but I was never in a rush to test the limits of that immortality. One Valkyrie would be more than a handful. Five Valkyrie was a death sentence.

I stepped into the oblivion circle.

"I thought you'd see it my way," Syght said with a small smile. "Please hold still."

She released the orb and it floated over to where I stood. It hovered a few inches away from my face and released white energy, which enveloped me. After several seconds, it floated back to Syght.

She repeated the process with each of us. A few minutes later, we were cleared to move to the other section of the lobby.

"What would've happened if we failed the orb test?" I asked as we moved past her desk.

"The circle would have activated and we'd be sweeping up your remains," Syght answered. "It might have been difficult to neutralize you, but your friends don't share your 'affliction' and would have been dispatched."

I shuddered at the thought.

"Hades isn't kidding with the security," I said as we headed to the elevators and two more Valkyrie escorts. "Are you serious?"

Corbel nodded. "No Valkyrie, no meeting Hades."

Both of our new Valkyrie tour guides wore identical dark blue suits. From the way the material rested on their bodies, I could tell it was dragonscale.

The elevator arrived, the doors opening silently. We stepped inside the large car, with both Valkyrie bringing up the rear. Both of them stood several inches over my six feet and wore an expression of mild distaste when they looked at me.

I made the same face when I tasted rancid milk. I didn't approach them because I valued my limbs—

attached to my body. They both looked like ripping off an arm or two would be light work. Their expressions softened for half a second while looking at Peaches.

<Do you think they have meat?>

<Boy, even if they did, I wouldn't dare ask. They look angry.>

<Did you make bad air? Their faces look like you made bad air.>

<No. I think they're always angry. They're warriors, Valkyrie.>

<Do Valkyries eat meat?>

<I think so, but I'm not asking. I'll get Monty to make you some upstairs.>

<They feel nice. Maybe if you lick them they will give you meat?>

<If I lick one of them, I'm pretty sure it'll be the last thing I attempt to lick—ever.>

<That's because your saliva doesn't heal. Should I lick them? >

<How about we save your amazing saliva for later? I'm pretty sure Monty is going to need healing, and then you can use extra saliva on him.>

Peaches shook his body, and for a brief second I thought the cables of the elevator were in danger of snapping.

"I'm going to say this, even though I think I'm wasting my breath," Corbel started. "Hades is in a foul mood. Strong, do you think it's possible you could let Tristan do all the talking?"

"Are you saying—?"

"Yes," Corbel interrupted. "In fact, I'd even prefer if you let the Hellhound speak before you opened your mouth to share."

"That almost sounds like you're saying I lack the ability to be tactful," I answered. "I'm fully aware Hades is worried and angry. Contrary to your belief, I do know how to deal with these kinds of situations."

"You've dealt with angry gods whose wives have been kidnapped before?"

"Well, not exactly kidnapped goddesses," I said. "Mrs. Hades is a goddess right?"

Corbel sighed and rubbed his face. "Why? Why do I even bother?"

TWELVE

MONTY STOOD OFF to the side, lost in thought. I had an idea what he was thinking. Why would someone move against Hades? Persephone was no slouch. Hades might have kidnapped her, but that didn't make her a soft target.

Whoever managed to grab her had to be powerful enough to subdue and transport a goddess. Could the Lucent have that much power? Stopping an entropy round with your face was one thing. Seizing a goddess was another.

How did Hades get so many Valkyrie? It wasn't like they were just hanging around Valhalla, lounging and doing nothing. Why would Odin invest himself in a cross-pantheon partnership? Last I remember, Odin wasn't exactly the sharing type.

I could've been mistaken. Monty may have just been thinking about a great cup of tea. It was hard to read him sometimes.

None of that explained why Syght and the Dark Council were involved. If she was running magical security for Hades, it meant the Dark Council had an interest in what was going on.

Corbel was right about one thing. Syght was a respected mage from the Dark Council. To have her down here, bouncing the door to the building, meant they were expecting some high-powered gatecrashers.

Then there was still the item Corbel went back to fetch. I giggled inside for a few seconds at my choice of words. I made a mental note to use that as soon as possible.

What was so important that Corbel would risk another trip to The Eldorado after facing Alnit?

We arrived at the top floor, and the Valkyrie stepped off, allowing us to exit the elevator. Set on the wall opposite the elevator was the Terra Sur logo. This one was done in stainless steel.

The Valkyrie entered the elevator and descended, as Corbel led us down the long hallway. There was only one large double door on this floor, and I could feel the energy emanating from it, even from this distance.

"What? No Valkyrie escort to the inner sanctum?" I asked as Corbel placed a hand on the door. "I'm disappointed."

"No need," Corbel said. "You'll see."

Runes shifted, interlocked, and separated. The rune-covered doors, which were at least six inches thick and made of Buloke ironwood, swung open with a sigh.

Inside, standing to either side of the doors, I counted ten super Valkyrie, five on each wall. The Valkyrie downstairs and outside were dangerous, but these made them look like lightweights. On the shoulder of each Valkyrie sat a black raven. Not as large as Herk, Dex's raven companion, but definitely leaning toward the industrial size.

The Valkyrie were easily seven feet tall, dressed in full-runed chainmail, and exuded generous amounts of badassery. All of them stood at attention, holding a broadsword pointed down in front of their bodies.

For a brief second, I thought they were statues. The ravens were motionless, which made me wonder if they weren't just office decoration, especially at this larger size. I stepped close to one of them and was about to poke it in the head, when a soft cough stopped me.

"Still looking to test the extent of your immortality?"

It was Hades.

At the far end of the hangar converted into an office was another redwood-sized desk. On both walls to either side of the desk were large screens, broken up into several dozen displays.

The desk itself held two clusters of monitors, made up of nine screens each. The fourth wall, behind the desk, consisted of one massive window-wall. The evening accentuated the lights of the skyline looking north. Another Terra Sur logo adorned the right wall, complete with an unbelievable diamond.

"Are those things real?" I asked, pointing to the super Valkyrie. Knowing Hades, it was possible the armor was empty and just for show. "Or is this just sleight-of-hand, Hades-style?"

Hades steepled his fingers, smiled, and sat back.

"I can assure you, they are real," Hades said. "Would you like to test their authenticity?"

"No, thank you," Monty said, glaring at me. "We have more pressing concerns."

Monty ignored me as we trekked across another large Persian rug. This one dwarfed the one in the lobby, covering the floor of the office from wall to wall. My feet sank into it as we walked. By the time we were close to the desk, my calves burned from the exertion. It was like walking on sand.

"Would it kill you to install tatami mats?" I asked, fighting my way through the rug. "Or something that doesn't feel like trekking across the Sahara?"

"You're stepping on a one-of-a-kind Kashan that I had custom made for this office," Hades replied. "I'm afraid they don't come in easily traversable models."

Behind the massive desk sat Hades. No matter how many times I encountered him, I never grew used to the *plainness* he exhibited. There was no godly smoke or lightning surrounding him, much to my disappointment.

Tonight he wore a dark gray Stuart Hughes bespoke, that—even minus the diamonds—cost more than all my suits combined. His gray Armani shirt had a hint of rose in it and was complemented by a blood-red Ricci diamond-plated tie.

I glanced over at Monty. "I'm sensing a trend here," I muttered under my breath as we sat in Hades' ridiculously overpriced wingback chairs. "You two should definitely schedule a shopping spree—maybe go bankrupt on High Street."

Hades sported his usual goatee and wore his moderately long hair against his shoulders. He looked like any other successful CEO of a large multinational corporation.

With one exception.

He was a god, and he was pissed.

THIRTEEN

MY SENSE OF self-preservation kicked in early and hard.

The energy coming off Hades was palpable, and it felt decidedly lethal. Corbel stepped over to Hades' side of the desk.

"Did you find it?" Hades asked him.

Corbel nodded and placed a small silver case on the desk. Monty narrowed his eyes, his expression growing dark. It was made with onyx inlays and was elegantly designed with silver filigree on each of the corners. I could see the runes inscribed on its surface glowing softly.

"That looks like a keepsaker," I said, remembering the box that was used to hold Redrum. "What is that?"

"Is that a—?" Monty began, the surprise evident in his voice.

"We'll get to this in a second," Hades said, resting a hand on the case. "Tell me what you discovered."

"We went back for a silver jewelry case?" I asked, upset.

"Not silver," Monty said. "Charonite—a soulkeeper."

"Very good, mage," Hades said with a nod, tapping the small case. "This is indeed charonite."

"I risked my life with a zigziggy for some jewelry in a 'charonite' case?"

Monty shook his head, and Hades smiled.

It was the kind of smile that promised a painful and prolonged death. Like when you swim out into shark-infested waters with an open wound. You know it's only a matter of time before it's over.

"A syzygy?" Hades asked, raising an eyebrow and looking at Corbel. "Is this true?"

Corbel nodded. "The second time we went back, after the explosion—"

"Explosion?" Hades asked, looking at me. "What *explosion*? Is The Eldorado still standing?"

"These two reconfigured the runes in the residence to detonate," Corbel answered, glancing at us. "Tristan used an entropic sequence, which preserved the building but destroyed the tower."

"Do you two have some pent-up anger issues you haven't addressed?" Hades asked. "Not enough hugs as children?"

I raised my hands in surrender. "I don't know about any entropic anything," I said. "That lightsaber, Walnut the First, triggered the runes and blasted the tower."

Hades looked over at Monty. "Can you translate?"

"We felt it prudent to visit Persephone's home first before meeting you," Monty started, "in order to discover a motive for her disappearance."

"I have enemies, mage," Hades said, his voice hard. "That is motive enough."

I shook my head. "This is true," I said, glancing at the silver case. "Someone wanted you to make a move, get you vulnerable."

"We encountered one of the Lucent, Alnit the First," Monty said, tapping his chin and staring at Hades. "But you knew this. You *knew* we'd go to The Eldorado first."

"It's the first thing I would've done," Hades answered. "The first place I would look."

"You sent us your Hound to spring the trap that you *knew* was in place?"

"Like I said, I have enemies," Hades replied. "The Lucent are only an instrument—a blunt one at that. I need to know who is wielding them."

"And he made it seem like it was our idea," I whispered. "I really dislike gods."

"I'm sure you'll be pleased to know many of them are not overly fond of the Montague & Strong Detective Agency," Hades answered. "Starting with a certain Hindu god of death."

"Shiva?" I asked. "He can go suck—"

"I was referring to Kali," Hades said. "Have you two spoken recently?"

"Oh, *her*," I said. "We aren't exactly on speaking terms."

"Yet, you are known as the 'chosen of Kali' in certain disreputable circles," Hades said. "I wonder why she chose you. Would you like to ask her?"

"Pass," I said quickly. "The last time we spoke, she was busy flinging curses around."

Hades nodded. "I understand your reluctance," he said. "It *will* have to happen eventually. You *do* realize they are linked?"

"Let's revisit that in a few centuries," I said. "Not eager to see either of them again for a few eons, if I can help it."

"Hades, the ones who took Persephone," Monty started, "do you know what they want?"

"*They* want what they have always wanted," Hades answered. "Power—and to eliminate me, if possible."

"Last time, they tried to blow you to hell"—I looked around the office again—"nice renovation, by the way. This time, they kidnap your wife. Seems personal."

"I don't make impersonal enemies, Strong. I control the Underworld. Within that domain are artifacts and items of immeasurable power. Items anyone, god or human, would kill for, many times over. Items I keep out of their hands."

"An enemy who would attempt to confront you would have to possess considerable power," Monty added. "Even to face you indirectly."

Hades stood and looked out of the window-wall.

"Open the case, mage," Hades said, looking out over the city. "That should provide some insight."

"Sir," Corbel said, "are you sure that's proper? I mean—?"

Hades raised a hand and Corbel fell silent.

"Why don't you show our Dark Council representative in?"

"Dark Council representative?" I asked, glancing at Monty. "Since when do you deal with the Council?"

"Since my wife was kidnapped in their jurisdiction," Hades answered without turning around. "She's the one who enjoys being on the surface among humans."

Corbel bowed and left the room. I looked at Monty, who hadn't moved.

"Are you going to open it?" I asked. "He said it was okay."

I saw Monty hesitate. This meant that whatever was in the charonite case was dangerous enough to make him pause.

"Whose essence is contained within?" Monty asked.

"You're right to be wary, mage," Hades said, turning to face Monty. "A soulkeeper, when active, is a powerful artifact."

"How powerful?" I asked, now concerned. "Powerful enough that we should leave the building before he opens it?"

"It's not explosive," Monty said under his breath. "At least I don't recall reading that they were. They have been known to undo the person opening them."

"Undo, as in unmake and disintegrate?"

"That is the definition of 'undo' I'm familiar with," Monty said, reaching for the case. "This one is active, but masking the essence contained within."

"Is that why Walnut couldn't find it?" I asked, looking at Hades. "Whose essence is in there?"

Hades reached over and touched the surface of the case with his index finger, letting energy flow into it.

"Tristan, do you know the sequence?"

Monty nodded, letting the case rest in his palm as energy pulsed across its surface. I moved my hand to my mala bracelet in case we needed a shield. I didn't trust Hades, and if this soulkeeper exploded, I wanted to have some kind of protection.

"Soulkeepers," Monty began, "are similar to the

keepsakers with sequential locks. Most of them have universal keys to make it easy for any mage above a certain level to open them."

"So this is basically a lock that every mage has a key to?" I asked. "Really? Some genius mage thought *that* was a good idea?"

"The mage must be of a certain level and given authorization to open the lock," Hades said. "Which I just granted."

I grabbed the mala bead and stood up. I didn't materialize my shield, but I was ready.

"You're going to excuse me if I'm not exactly comfortable with the whole 'this isn't an explosive case' scenario."

"That's not necessary, Strong," Hades said. "Soulkeepers do *not* explode."

Monty whispered something under his breath and touched the four corners of the case in a predetermined sequence.

The fact that he knew the order, or that he even knew the case was a soulkeeper, only demonstrated how much I didn't know about this world I had been violently shoved into.

For a few seconds, nothing happened. Monty put the case down on the desk again.

"Are you certain it's active?" Monty asked. "The delay seems long."

"I may not be a mage," I said, "but I've watched enough to know when the artifact starts to act strange, it's time to exit the premises."

The runes on the surface started glowing brighter. I pressed the bead on my mala, creating my shield.

Peaches whined next to me.

<Do you smell something?>

<That box. It's starting to smell bad.>

That was enough confirmation for me.

"What are you doing?" Hades asked. "It's reacting to the sequence."

"I've learned a few things in my short time in the world of gods, dragons and magic," I answered, moving back and keeping the shield in front of me. "When someone, usually a god, says don't worry—worry. Worry your ass off."

The runes became brighter, and Hades picked up the soulkeeper. "It's harmless, Strong," Hades said. "Soulkeepers are a type of runic vault, designed to safekeep the essence of an individual. In this case, my wife, Persephone."

"The other thing I've learned," I said, making sure Peaches was behind the shield and me. "Is that when a Montague says something isn't explosive, it usually is—in a spectacular way."

Hades smiled and shook his head. Monty must have sensed something, because he stood and came to my side. The super Valkyrie along the walls shifted as one, turning to face Hades and the rear wall.

"That's not creepy at all," I said, noticing the increase in ambient energy in the office. "I doubt they are picking up on how 'harmless' that case is. I don't think my shield is going to be enough."

"The runes do appear to be increasing in intensity," Monty said, grabbing the edge of my shield and gesturing. "It appears someone, or something, has tampered with that soulkeeper."

"Impossible," Hades said, grabbing the lid of the case and opening it. "This soulkeeper has been hidden and untouched. I hid it myself. It's perfectly sa—"

Monty dropped a golden lattice around us as the soulkeeper exploded.

FOURTEEN

MY SHIELD EVAPORATED in the blast.

The energy wave rushed around us, destroying everything in its path. The super Valkyrie standing against the walls raised their swords and created a shield.

It lasted for a good five seconds.

The swords broke first, destroying their shield. This was followed by pieces of chainmail being ripped off and disintegrated. Monty cast a teleportation circle behind the Valkyrie.

"Inside!" he yelled and pointed behind them. "Now! Evacuate the building!"

The Valkyrie knew when to exit a lethal blast and ran for the circle, disappearing a few seconds later, along with the circle itself. The energy from the soulkeeper increased with a roar, undoing the lattice around us.

"Monty," I said, trying to reactivate my shield, "that looks bad. Can we teleport out of here?"

"Too much interference," he yelled. "The increased energy of the blast is preventing any further casting."

<Boy, can you take us somewhere else?>

<I can't. The wind doesn't let me go in-between.>

So much for the Hellhound teleport.

The sound around us was deafening. It felt like standing on a subway platform and having ten NYC subway trains entering the station at once. The floor beneath us vibrated as the items around the office were consumed by the energy swirling around us. We were sitting in a tornado of power that was chewing up everything in its path.

Behind the desk, holding the soulkeeper, stood a frozen Hades. He appeared to be fighting—and losing—against the wave of power rushing around him. His suit had been shredded, along with what remained of his desk.

Closing the lid and wrapping the case in his massive fists, he tried to contain the energy. For a brief moment, it appeared he had it under control, before the case blasted open again and shattered the window-wall behind Hades.

I looked past Hades, and my blood froze. In the distance, standing on the roof of an adjacent building, I saw Alnit the First, gesturing. I tugged on Monty's arm, getting his attention.

"What is he doing?" I yelled.

White runes floated from Alnit's fingers for a few moments, and then raced at Hades. A white lattice wrapped itself around the god of the Underworld. With a look of surprise, he clawed at it but couldn't remove the net of energy enveloping him.

On another adjacent building, I saw a second figure, Lucent Two, dressed identically to Alnit. This one gestured and created a black orb of angry energy. He released it and it floated over to our building.

It stopped just outside the shattered window and transformed into a black swirling mass. It was unlike any portal I'd ever seen.

"Monty," I yelled. "They're trying to grab him!"

Movement caught my eye, and I looked up. Above us floated a third figure, Lucent Three, dressed like the other two. This one held an orb the size of the Unisphere above his head.

The orb shifted between red and black. Bright beams of orange and yellow coruscated across its surface. It reminded me of the orb that had melted the Goat. Only this was the industrial-sized version.

Lucent Three just floated there with his arms outstretched over his head and, for a second, I thought he was going to ask the other two to lend him their energy. I pointed, and Monty visibly paled. This meant I nearly shit my pants.

"Bloody hell," Monty said. "That is bad."

"What?" I asked, feeling everything about this situation was bad. "What is bad?"

"Do you recall what happened to the Goat?" Monty asked, gesturing faster than I'd ever seen him move. "When the Ghost Magistrate reduced it to slag?"

I nodded, not wanting to hear the rest of what he was explaining. Nothing good could come after that question.

"Is that—?"

"Going to do the same thing to this building," Monty finished. "If we don't stop it."

"Stop it?" I asked, realizing my grip on sanity was

slipping. "Are you crazy? We can't stop that thing! It's bigger than the building."

"The size is irrelevant, but I'm going to need your help."

"What about Hades?"

"Forget me," Hades said, glancing behind him. "Find her and bring her back to me."

"He's trapped," Monty said, shaking his head. "Even I can't break that lattice. We'll have to catch up to him later."

"You know where that portal leads?"

"I have an idea, yes, but we need to focus," Monty said, pausing the gestures. "Your magic missile."

"My what?" I asked. "You can't be serious. Are we committing suicide today?"

"And your blade," he said, holding out a hand. "When I tell you, you cast your magic missile at that orb."

"At that ginormous, building-melting orb?" I asked, handing him Ebonsoul. "My puny, mostly malfunctioning, missile?"

"Once they take Hades, they'll try to erase us," Monty said, rolling up a sleeve, running the edge of Ebonsoul along his forearm and drawing blood. "We have about three seconds to act. Don't miss."

"Miss? That orb is the only thing in the sky," I snapped. "It *is* the sky right now."

"Which makes it easier for you," Monty said, tracing runes on his arm in blood. "Get ready."

"What are you doing?" I said, looking at the runes glow with energy along his arm. "You're using blood magic?"

"I'm giving us a chance to survive this," Monty answered, his voice grim. "It's the only way now."

"They *will* come after you for this, Montague," Hades said. "When they do, know you have an ally in me."

"What is he talking about? Who will come after you?"

Monty glared at Hades. "He's delirious," Monty replied. "That lattice is sapping his energy and making him speak gibberish. Remember, as soon as Hades is gone, fire your missile."

"Be aware, Simon, in order to sabotage the soulkeeper, someone had to know of its hiding place," Hades said, his voice hard. "That is a small group. Start there."

"How are you still giving orders?" I asked. "You're about to be taken who knows where on a lattice express."

"The mage knows," Hades replied. "Find her, and then come find me. You'll know where to look."

The lattice tightened around Hades' body, yanked him back and out of the office, through the shattered window and into the portal.

The swirling energy around us stopped. I looked around the warzone that used to be the office. Everything was either already completely destroyed, or on its way to total disintegration.

The silence was deafening.

That's when I felt the shift, and looked up. Lucent Three was saying something into the night. I couldn't make out the words, but I was pretty certain it wasn't anything pleasant.

It was probably something along the lines of 'time to

die,' or 'eat my orb and disintegrate, you rat bastards.' Either way, I knew that what was coming next promised pain.

FIFTEEN

"NOW, SIMON."

"IGNIS VITAE," I said under my breath. The violet orb that formed in my palm was small, only about three inches across, but the energy it contained was overwhelming. I had to avert my gaze to avoid being blinded.

I extended my arm, but the orb wouldn't budge. I shook my hand, but it was stuck.

"What the hell?" I said, trying to shake the orb off. "Monty?"

"Apologies," he said. "I placed a limiter on your spell to make sure you didn't release it before it was time."

"You didn't think it was a good idea to tell me that?"

"I just did," he said, returning Ebonsoul. "You should be feeling a surge any moment."

"A surge?" I felt Ebonsoul siphon power into me from Monty. "That's from you?"

"You're welcome," he said with a short nod, a grimace, and a quick glance down at my thigh sheath. "That should give you an additional boost. I'm curious, is there a reason you're using a sheath for your blade?"

"It's complicated," I said quickly. "I've had a few 'issues' trying to materialize it after my last session with Yat."

"Issues?" Monty asked. "What kind of issues? This sounds serious."

"Nothing serious," I answered, raising a hand. "Just prefer to wear it in a sheath for now."

I forgot how observant Monty was. I didn't think he'd notice, and then, I remembered: mages are detail-oriented, and Monty could be OCD when it came down to picking up details.

"Your bond is changing, isn't it?"

"You make it sound like I'm going through puberty," I said.

"That's not entirely inaccurate," he answered. "If you consider your use of energy, and—"

"Drop it," I said, before he got into Montypedia mode. "We can discuss this later. If there is a later."

Monty narrowed his eyes and stared at me for a few seconds. I knew that look. He'd let it go—for now.

"Consider it dropped," he said with a nod. "You really should brace yourself. Your blade siphoned a considerable amount of energy."

Dahvina's words came back to me: *"Hellhound, Kali, and this blade. You're thrice-bound, and two of your bonds are so intertwined, I don't know if they can be separated."*

The truth was, that the bond with Ebonsoul was changing. I had since learned that it was joined to my bond with Peaches. As that bond evolved, my bond to the blade shifted.

Whatever the cause, it was getting harder to retrieve

it from its silvery-mist form. Even in the sheath, I felt the tug of its power. It wanted to be inside of me, and that's *exactly* why I wore it in the sheath.

It was my conversation with Nana that had made me change my mind about the whole silvery mist storage mode.

"Has this weapon spoken to you?"

"No, it doesn't speak to me."

"That's good. The essence of this blade is dangerous and bloodthirsty," she said. "That's one part of the bond you don't need."

Last thing I needed was my blade encouraging me to go on a killing spree. Ebonsoul had never spoken to me and I intended to keep it that way. I figured if I kept my blade in a sheath, it would limit any and all conversations.

If I was going to carry a dangerous, bloodthirsty blade, it was going to sit in a sheath on my thigh, not joined inside my body in silvery mist form. I had no intention of waking up one day and calling Ebonsoul 'my precious.'

Besides, constant conversations with a ravenous Hellhound, in addition to my own inner voice telling me to find a nice, deserted island and retire, was all the head chatter I could mentally handle. If I added one more voice, Monty would have to find me a nice, comfortable room in Bellevue.

Another wave of energy slammed into me, making me gasp. Monty had grown stronger—much stronger. The increase in his life force must have been a result of his recent shift.

"Are you crazy?" I asked. "This is your life force! We

can't do this!"

"We have to. It's the only way."

"There has to be another way. This is too much power."

"Did you forget what we are facing? The Lucent just snatched a *god*."

"I'm not going to let you sacrifice yourself to save all of us," I said, even though he had a point. Snatching a god definitely kicked the Lucent up in the badass category. "Maybe we can call in the Dark Council."

"Who said anything about sacrificing myself?" he shot back. "I'm a mage, not a martyr. I'm channeling energy into your anemic magic missile in order for us to survive this. I don't plan on dying in this oversized tribute to a god's ego Hades calls an office."

I grimaced in pain as my body flushed hot to deal with the damage. His idea of channeling energy felt like pouring boiling water over my skin.

"It's too much," I said. "It feels like my arm is about to explode. I can't do this, let go."

"Just a little longer. It's either this or we end up like the Goat."

"Why would they want to destroy the entire building? They already have Hades and Persephone, I'm guessing. Why the obliteration?"

"Cover their tracks?" Monty answered. "Prevent us from following them? Melting an entire building is quite a distraction."

"I'm already feeling like I'm melting from the inside. I need to release this thing."

"Not yet," Monty said, clenching his teeth. He placed his blood-smeared hand on the orb. It transformed from violet to blood-red. The energy increased, threatening to shred my body. The pain ratcheted up a few notches into 'drive a spike into my ear and hit it with a hammer' level.

"Have I told you how much I hate mages right now?"

Monty grabbed my hand and extended my arm toward the window. I heard him muttering something under his breath, and I felt another surge of energy race up my arm.

The orb increased in size. It went from three inches to about a foot in diameter. Black energy raced across Monty's arm as the runes on his forearm became black and I saw the blood burn off.

"What are you doing?" I asked in alarm. "This spell is too dangerous. We have to stop."

"If we stop, that orb will hit this building and kill everyone, including you," Monty said, holding my arm in place. "You may come back, but everyone inside is going to die."

I stood, transfixed, as Lucent Three brought both arms down and vanished. Alnit and Lucent Two had disappeared when Hades was yanked into the black portal. The building-melting orb slowly descended.

"I think now would be a good time to let it go, don't you agree, Monty?"

"Not yet, they may be watching. If we try to stop it too early, they could interfere and prevent us from saving the building."

"Well," I said through clenched teeth, "it's definitely a change of pace. We've gone from destroying buildings to trying to save one. Ramirez would be proud. That orb is getting really close."

"Not yet. I need to make sure we don't miss. We have only one opportunity. If we miss, it's over."

"I could literally aim in any direction and still not miss," I said as tears of pain streamed down my face. My body was barely keeping up with the damage inflicted by the spell. "Can we do this before I pass out?"

I saw the orb getting closer and, just when I thought it was too late, Monty released even more energy. The skin on his arm began to smoke and I could see him wince in pain. His suit jacket began to smolder and smoke as scorch marks appeared in several locations.

"There goes another jacket," he said with a grimace. "Piero is going to be absolutely livid."

"Monty, we need to stop. If you keep this up, you're going to lose your arm."

"A few more seconds."

I heard Peaches whine next to me.

<That energy smells bad.>

<I know, boy, but we're going to stop it right now—as soon as Monty lets me fire this magic missile.>

<Your magic doesn't really work.>

<I'm not a mage, but I can use some magic.>

<Maybe you should make some healthy sausage, and I can fire some bad air at it.>

<I'm trying to concentrate here. You eating healthy sausage would probably be more dangerous than that orb coming at us. Let me focus.>

<Just an idea, since your magic needs a lot of practice. I think your focus should be on meat. Every Hellhound knows…Meat is Life.>

Apparently, everyone around me thought they were comedians. Part of me felt that Peaches was right. My magic was faulty at best. Even with the enhancements Monty had just provided, I had a feeling this wasn't going to end well.

"Now, Simon," Monty said, gripping my arm. "Release it."

Monty muttered another series of words I couldn't understand, and I released the magic missile. It flew up into the large orb with a violet streak behind it.

"It's best if we put some distance between us and that orb," Monty said, heading for the door. "Now would be ideal."

"You don't want to stick around and admire your handiwork?" I asked, looking up at the enormous orb of death. "I mean, we have front-row seats."

"This is not front-row seating. If my calculations are even slightly off, this becomes ground zero."

"What's that mean? I thought the Monty-enhanced magic missile would be enough to stop it?"

"I used *blood magic*," Monty said. "I'm not exactly well-versed in dark magic. It has a tendency to be unstable in the best of circumstances. Not to mention, I interlaced the cast with entropic properties."

"What is it with you and entropy?" I asked, worried he would so easily resort to dark magic. It was becoming a dangerous trend. "What do you mean you laced the cast with entropic properties?"

"Do you recall the void vortex?"

"Which, the first or the second one?"

He gave me a short glare, easily a three on the Eastwood glare-o-meter. "So glad you've maintained that cutting wit in the face of impending doom."

"It's a gift," I said as we ran down the hallway. "Yes, I remember. What about them?"

"If this goes wrong, most of lower Manhattan will be reduced to a memory."

"I'm curious…" I said, as my heart started doing a double-time fandango at the loss of life if we messed up. "Are you trying to destroy the city? Did you forget that the last time you cast a void vortex, the Golden Circle had a shit-fit, and put out an APB on you?"

"APB?"

"Assassinate Psychotic Brit, with extreme prejudice, I might add."

"I do not suffer from psychosis," Monty replied, irritated.

"Right, you just have a particular way of thinking and perceiving reality that's different from everyone else."

"That's one way of defining it," he said, opening the stairwell door. "By now, you must have gathered that all mages harbor some kind of instability."

"Present company excluded?"

"Of course. Now that my uncle is overseeing things at the Golden Circle, we shouldn't expect any magistrates after us."

"*Us*? I'm not the mage, *you* are."

"And yet, *I* helped *you* with this cast."

"Well, shit."

"Indeed," Monty answered. "If they send magistrates, they will have a few questions for you—of the violent sort."

I was about to respond, when I realized he was right. If any magistrates came after us, there was a good chance they would be targeting me this time. Monty was almost 'Hades-level' scary with his plans.

"Why does this feel like you set me up?"

"I would not resort to such subterfuge," Monty said, gesturing as we descended. "I really hope those Valkyrie were able to evacuate the building in time."

"No, you'd just blatantly set me up."

"This wasn't a 'setup'," he said. "Your missile didn't possess the power to stop that orb without my assistance. Consider this field training."

Every few steps, an orange, rune-covered shield would materialize behind us, covering the entire stairwell.

"How are we going to know if my magic missile worked?"

"Your missile should be making impact any second now," Monty said, releasing another shield. "If it works, we'll still be here twenty seconds after that. If not, we won't."

"I just want to say," I said, as we raced downstairs, "the mage method of testing things really sucks."

"Welcome to the world of magic, where the room for error is usually fatal," he said as the air became charged around us. "That would be the impact of your magic missile. Brace yourself."

A low, rumbling sound washed over us and the building began to shake. Next thing I knew, all of the power had been cut, and we stood in a darkened stairwell waiting for the end.

SIXTEEN

THE END NEVER arrived.

Twenty seconds later, we weren't atomized, which meant the blood magic-missile had worked. Monty raised a hand and released a light orb to allow us to descend without tripping and breaking our necks.

We continued downstairs until we reached the lobby. I opened the door and found the reception area, including the security desk, empty of personnel. What used to be the oblivion circle was now a scorched mess.

"Seems the Valkyrie managed to get everyone out in time," I said, noticing that even the Valkyrie outside the building were gone. "That was pretty thorough, don't you think?"

"It would seem that way," Monty said, looking around. "I'd be curious to see who the Dark Council representative was."

"I think it's more important that we locate Hades," I answered. "Don't you think that's kind of the priority right now? He said you may have an idea of where that portal led."

"I do, but first we need to track down who would target Hades and why."

"Who benefits from his absence and how?"

"Precisely," Monty said. "Getting Hades out of the way must serve a purpose."

"You heard him," I replied. "God of the Underworld? Lots of enemies. Isn't Tartarsauce one of these enemies?"

"*Tartarus* is usually oblivious to what humans and gods are doing," Monty replied, correcting me. "His attention would be on larger matters. He feels we are beneath him, like ants to a human."

"Unless you get swarmed by a column of African safari ants," I answered. "Those are hard to ignore."

"Point taken," Monty said. "We'll have to be like the mighty *siafu* in this context, and goad him from below."

"Except *he's* really below us?"

"Technically correct," Monty said, looking around. "Where did they cast?"

"Where did who cast?"

"Are you familiar with the Tomatis effect?"

"The tomato effect?" I asked, confused. "Why are we discussing tomatoes?"

"The *Tomatis* effect. Not tomatoes. Are you even listening?"

"Never heard of it. Is he a mage?"

"No," Monty said, still searching the floor. "Alfred Tomatis was a scientist who worked with auditory properties and therapy."

"He worked with how people hear?"

Monty nodded. "Specifically with something called auditory zoom," Monty answered. "The way a crowded room can sound noisy until you pinpoint on a voice."

"Are you sure he wasn't a mage?"

"Certain," Monty said. "Like the Tomatis effect with hearing and auditory zoom, mages have a similar effect with energy called a runic zoom."

"Which is?"

"Mages can pinpoint different energy signatures, depending on who is doing the casting."

"Is this another Ziller thing?"

"You do realize," Monty said, tracing runes around another scorched space on the floor, "that there are other mages besides Professor Ziller?"

"Really? I just thought this was going to be another Zillerfication of the runic auditory mage senses. Or maybe he wrote a book on the subject: *Quantum Mechanics of the Inner Ear—How Earwax Affects Balance and Casting*."

"I'll make sure to share how highly you think of his work the next time we meet," Monty said, finishing his gesturing. "Here, they tried to hide it. This signature is familiar somehow, but I can't pinpoint it."

"What's that?" I asked, as another circle formed on the floor in the middle of the scorched-out area. "Another oblivion circle?"

"This is a teleportation circle, disguised to look like an oblivion circle." Monty placed a hand on the edge of the circle. "Someone left here in a hurry. I don't recognize who it was, but if I encounter them again, I will."

"You can pinpoint certain energy signatures?"

"Yes, it takes years of practice. Older mages can do it almost reflexively. This one feels familiar, but it's off, like something is missing."

"Ah, so you're saying you're old. I did see you move kind of stiffly up in Hades' office," I said, wiggling my fingers. "Fingers getting slower? Pain in the joints? No shame in aging, you know."

"We need to determine if it's really Tartarus controlling the Lucent," Monty said, ignoring me, "or if this is a little closer to home."

"But the Lucent serve him," I said. "If they're involved, are they working for Tartarus?"

"The Dark Council may be able to give us insight into who is behind this," Monty said, removing his ruined jacket with a look of disgust. His shirt didn't look much better, but I refrained from mentioning it. Monty was a bit touchy about his wardrobe. "If Syght was scanning for security, you can rest assured that Erik knows what's going on."

"Hellfire Club?"

"Either that or I need to arrange a meeting with Erik."

"Let's do that," I said. "Erik creeps me out in his mage S&M dungeon. Does he ever get out?"

"Can you sense anyone else?" Monty asked, scanning the lobby.

I closed my eyes and let my senses expand. From what I could tell, the building was empty. What surprised me was how a small group of Valkyrie could evacuate a ten-story building in such a short amount of time.

"Do you really think ten of those super Valkyrie could evacuate everyone in this building, even if it was sparsely occupied?"

Monty rubbed his chin. "I find that unlikely. The more probable scenario is that only Hades' office and the lobby were occupied, with a large contingent of Valkyrie security."

"It's almost like he expected this," I said.

"He kept the building empty...deliberately. The energy signatures I sensed earlier could have been false."

"I was thinking the same thing, which means Hades was using himself—"

"As bait," Monty finished. "Why would the god of the Underworld let himself be captured?"

"He was expecting the Lucent, but he wanted to show us something as well. I'm just not seeing it."

"The lattice that immobilized him was stronger than anything I have encountered," Monty said. "I just don't know if it was strong enough to stop a god."

"You don't think it was stronger than Hades?"

"Unlikely," Monty said. "It was definitely beyond my capabilities of unraveling, but Hades manipulates power on a scale that's nearly unimaginable."

I looked around the empty lobby.

"And where is Mr. Hound of Hades?" I asked. "He went to get the Dark Council rep and never found his way back to the office?"

"We have clues, but we can't stand here and try to decipher them," Monty said. "We need to move. It's possible the Lucent will return."

"Why would they come back? They have what they wanted."

"Do they?" Monty asked as we headed out of the building. "It's possible that Hades is only a means to an end."

I turned to look at the building and stopped in shock. "I thought we were 'saving' the building?"

Monty glanced up. "We saved most of it," he said matter-of-factly. "They can always rebuild. I'm sure the foundation is strong."

The newly named and renovated Terra Sur Global building, which was once ten-stories tall, had been neatly reduced to a five-story blown-out husk.

"Half the building is gone," I said, scanning the property. "You know we're just going to get blamed for more destruction."

"Yes, but in this case, *you* are responsible for this destruction."

"Me? How am I responsible?" I asked, confused. "The Lucent fired the building-melter. All I did—with *your* help, I might add—was stop it from reducing the building to dust."

"True," Monty said, tugging on one of his ruined shirt sleeves, "but if you had let it run its course, there would be no building to blame us for."

"*You* suggested stopping the spell!" I said, losing my patience. "Are you saying we could have just let it happen?"

"Well, yes," Monty replied, scanning the front of the building. "There was that small detail about everyone in the building dying. Including us."

"Save a building or save the lives," I said, my voice hard, processing the damage. "I'll pick lives every time."

"Agreed," Monty added. "In any case, I prefer to view it as half of the building still remains, not half of it is gone."

"Is that what you want me to say to Ramirez?" I asked incredulously. "It's not *that* bad, Angel. Don't look at it as half of the building is gone…no, see it as half of the building is still there."

"I'm sure he'll understand," Monty answered. "It's clear your magic missile still needs work."

"Excuse me?"

"If it were stronger, it would have impacted the orb earlier and stopped it before it destroyed the building."

"You're saying this is my fault?"

"I'm saying that, if you take the time to explain it to Director Ramirez, he'll understand why this happened," Monty replied. "You just need more practice."

"You must know a different Director Ramirez."

We walked across the plaza and headed to the Dark Goat. I unlocked the vehicle and let Peaches in the back seat. He immediately sprawled and rolled onto his back.

Monty stepped to the rear of the Dark Goat and removed a new suit from the cavern we called a trunk. It was spacious enough to hold a Hellhound in sprawl mode. I stood, transfixed, looking at the destroyed building.

Within seconds, Monty had changed his wardrobe and closed the trunk, when I felt an energy shift from behind us. I unholstered Grim Whisper and fired in the direction of the energy signature. After the Lucent, my new policy was shoot first and not even bother with questions.

I saw two figures step out of a side alley. One of them was hunched over and was being supported by the second.

I don't miss.

Either I shot the one that was hunched over, or someone was entropy-round proof. Monty formed a flame orb and entered a defensive position.

"Come out slowly," I said, keeping Grim Whisper trained on the figure that wasn't hunched over. "Or not, and I get to shoot you."

The tinkling of rounds hitting the street caught my attention. Someone, or better yet something, caught the entropy rounds I had fired earlier.

"That would not be the best course of action, considering we just thwarted several assassination attempts."

The voice was female. It was sultry and dangerous all at once, making my heart skip a few beats as I realized who was in the dark.

It was Michiko. She was wearing skintight Daystrider armor. It was enhanced UV repellant combat armor, designed to allow vampires to fight and move about during the day without taking damage from the sun.

Michiko's armor was black with a red dragon imprint encircling her body. Its head started at her shoulder, with the image of the dragon wrapping itself around her torso, the tail ending at a thigh.

"You were the Dark Council rep?"

"Holster your weapon, Strong," Corbel said. "I need your help".

"Helping you has become hazardous to my health," I said. "Where did you go?"

"I was escorting Ms. Nakatomi from the lobby, when we were attacked by a Lucent," Corbel answered with a grunt. "I can give you all the details later. Right now I think we need to pay a visit to the sorceress."

Chi stepped forward, holding up Corbel as he grabbed his midsection. His shirt and pants were soaked with blood, and I realized that if we didn't get him to Haven soon, there was a good chance the Hound of Hades wouldn't make it.

SEVENTEEN

"I THOUGHT YOU were impervious to everything," I said, racing uptown. "You're the Hound of Hades."

"Working for the god of the Underworld doesn't make me invincible," Corbel said with a groan. "It makes me dangerous."

I glanced back in the rearview mirror. Monty was casting, and a golden light suffused the back of the Dark Goat. Peaches had surrendered half of the back seat, which was a surprise in and of itself.

<Should I lick him? My saliva has healing properties.>

<I think we should let Monty cast his spell. If that doesn't work, then I guess we can let you lick him.>

<He doesn't look very good. Tell the angry man to let me lick him.>

I glanced over at Chi, locking eyes for a second, and realized we had a lot to discuss.

"Monty, how's it going back there?" I said, swerving through traffic and jumping onto 1st Avenue. "Can you fix him?"

"Damn it, Strong, I'm a mage, not a healer," Monty

snapped. "The spell I'm casting is not strong enough to deal with this wound. He's still bleeding."

I ignored the fact that he had just McCoyed me.

"Let Peaches help," I said. "He can heal him."

Both Monty and Chi give me a look.

"You want me to let your Hellhound help, *how*? Corbel isn't a sausage, you know. Does he happen to know a spell I'm not familiar with?"

"Trust me," I said. "Peaches can help."

Corbel reached up and grabbed Monty's hand.

"For once, Strong is right. Let the Hellhound help."

Monty stopped casting and moved to one side. Peaches leaned over Corbel, letting a low rumble escape. For the briefest of seconds, I thought my Hellhound was about to chomp on the guy.

Peaches planted himself in the back seat, spread his legs and shook his head. The Dark Goat swerved, and I almost fishtailed with his shaking.

<Stop shaking, boy.>

<I'm getting ready. Sometimes I have to shake.>

<Okay, but if you keep shaking, you're going to shake us into a wall.>

The runes along Peaches' body came to life. This time, they gave off a low violet glow, a color I'd never seen before. I made a mental note to ask him about that later, when we weren't dealing with someone bleeding out in the car.

Peaches placed his head over the wound and licked. The runes glowed brighter, and for second I thought he was going to go Peaches XL inside the Dark Goat. After ten seconds, he stopped licking. Monty looked at the wound and shook his head.

"I don't know how he did it, but the bleeding stopped," Monty said in disbelief. "Since when does Hellhound saliva contain healing properties?"

"I think it has something to do with our bond getting stronger, and the fact that he can become the size of a small bus."

"That's one good dog," Corbel said and passed out.

Monty looked down and examined the wound. "The saliva must possess a strong anesthetic," Monty said. "Corbel is unconscious. The knitting around the wound is worthy of the White Phoenix."

"We're about ten minutes out," I said. "You may want to call Roxanne and let her know we're coming in hot."

Monty pulled out his phone and dialed Haven. I heard him speaking to Roxanne, describing the wound.

"How did it happen?" I asked Chi. "I wasn't kidding when I said he was impervious to everything."

"He works *for* a god," she responded. "It doesn't make him immortal."

"I just figured with a title like the Hound of Hades…"

"What? That he was indestructible?" she asked, exasperated. "The blade that cut him was designed for that purpose."

She glanced down at the sheath that held Ebonsoul.

"Like mine?" I said under my breath. "I saw the blades the Lucent wield up close. They were a nasty piece of work."

"You faced a Lucent? And survived?"

"I got lucky," I replied. "His blade was the same as mine."

She shook her head slowly. "It's similar to yours, but much older. It predates your blade by several millennia."

"That blade…" I asked. "If it cuts me, will it—?"

"In my history, the blade used this evening is known as a *Kamikira*, a godkiller," Chi said, her voice hard. "These blades are not supposed to exist."

"I think Corbel would disagree with you."

"If you are injured by this blade," she said, glancing at me, "keep your Hellhound close. I don't know if your curse will save you."

I nodded. "Good thing we found you."

"Indeed," she replied. "Your creature may have saved his life."

<I think that deserves a sausage or ten.>

<I agree. Once we get out, I'll speak to Monty.>

"Roxanne will be waiting for us at the ambulance bay," Monty said from the back seat. "I explained the wound and the weapon, but I don't know what she'll be able to do. Maybe your vampire" —he looked at Chi— "can give Roxanne more insight."

Chi gave a short nod. "There are ways to combat this wound but you will not know of them," Chi said. "They require knowledge of the Darker Arts. I will help your woman."

For a moment, Monty was at a loss for words.

"She's not my—"

"You may deceive yourself, mage," Chi answered, glancing at me, "but this sorceress has marked you, whether or not you choose to believe it."

I pulled into the ambulance bay. Roxanne was standing by with a gurney and several medical techs. They removed Corbel from the Dark Goat and wheeled him into Haven.

I noticed the back seat wasn't covered in blood. I gave Monty a look, which he returned. The Dark Goat was officially becoming creepier.

"Simon, Tristan," Roxanne said, her voice crisp. "I see you've been keeping busy."

She exchanged a look with Monty, and then she ran after the gurney. "Third-floor, West Wing," she yelled as she helped push Corbel into the elevator.

As the elevator doors closed behind Roxanne, I turned to Chi.

"Why does the Dark Council care what happens to Hades?"

"Hades is a stabilizing force in the city. If he is removed, the void that is left behind will cause warring factions to destroy the city in an attempt to fill it."

"Sell that to someone else," I said, irritated. "The Dark Council doesn't care about Hades or any warring factions."

Monty raised an eyebrow as he looked at me. His expression was clear. It was along the lines of, 'so you've grown tired of breathing and have chosen death by vampire.'

Chi took a breath and let out a sigh, which was unnecessary considering she was undead.

"You're right, we don't care about Hades, or what he does with his companies," she answered, her voice ice. "We care about beings who can snatch an Olympian and who possess artifacts that can kill a god."

"The Lucent?"

"The ones controlling them."

I suddenly knew why she was the Dark Council

representative.

"You knew this could happen, that Hades was a target."

"After the initial attack, when Chaos was involved, we prepared contingencies," she replied. "These beings are the real threat."

Something was missing. She was giving me an answer but she was leaving something out. Hades' words came back to me: *I don't make impersonal enemies, Strong. I control the Underworld. Within that domain are artifacts and items of immeasurable power. Items anyone, god or human, would kill for, many times over. Items I keep out of their hands.*

Was it possible the Dark Council was after some of those artifacts? Or was Chi right, and they just wanted to keep the city safe from beings like the Lucent and Tartarus?

"What contingencies?" I asked. "Why are you here?"

"My purpose here this evening was to inform the god of the Underworld that he needed to secure his domain."

"And if he didn't?"

"Then," she said, staring into my eyes with an iron resolve, "the Dark Council would do it for him."

EIGHTEEN

WE HEADED UPSTAIRS to the third floor.

Corbel lay on a large bed with several medical personnel around him. I saw at least one doctor, in addition to Roxanne, working on the wound.

Roxanne looked up and noticed us but kept working. I saw dark energy form around her hands as she pressed them against Corbel.

Chi entered the room and spoke with Roxanne, while Monty and I stood outside. Roxanne nodded, gave the other doctor instructions, and shifted the energy in her hands from black to a deep red.

After a few minutes, Roxanne wiped the sweat from her brow, gave the other doctor some final instructions, and stepped outside.

Roxanne narrowed her eyes at Monty.

"You and I need to speak, Tristan Montague." Her tone let him know this was not a request. "Now."

"Corbel?" I asked as they walked away. "Will he make it?"

Roxanne shot me a glare that silenced any further

questions. The last thing I wanted was an angry sorceress blaming me for anything.

That look meant that, while she was pissed at Monty for something, she had plenty of anger to share. I didn't look forward to that conversation.

I felt Chi shift next to me. That was deliberate, since I knew she could move undetected if she wanted to.

"I think that Hades will survive his ordeal with the Lucent," Chi said. "However, the sorceress is concerned about your mage. His use of magic is…problematic."

"He's not my mage," I said. "It's not like I *own* him."

Chi raised an eyebrow. "He works for you, doesn't he?"

I let out a short sigh. "We work together. He doesn't work *for* me. We're partners."

She ran a finger along my cheek. "You are the immortal," she said. "He's just a mage, he should be working for you."

"He's not *just* anything," I said, grabbing her wrist and slowly removing it from my face. I made certain to make this a gentle gesture. I was still conscious of the fact that she was a vampire, an old and insanely powerful vampire. "He's my friend, he's my family."

"You can pick your friends, Simon," she replied. "You can't choose your family."

"You're wrong," I said with finality. "Monty would risk his life for me, and has done so on several dangerous occasions."

"Situations he himself has been the catalyst of."

"What are you trying to say?"

She looked up into my eyes. For someone who was undead, she smelled amazing.

"You know about the mark I placed on you," she said. "Once I gave you the blade, it was necessary to protect you. Ebonsoul makes you a target because of what it can do."

"So you're saying marking me was a method of protection?" I asked incredulously. "Not you claiming me as your property? Why didn't you just tell me?"

"You wouldn't have understood at the time."

"I don't understand now. Remove it."

"Only death can remove it."

My mind flashed to Ezra. "What do you mean 'only death' can remove it?" I asked. "Are you saying—?"

"The only way to remove the mark I have placed on you is by death—yours or mine."

"Do I look like some kind of dry-erase board where anyone can come leave their mark? So this is really til death do us part?"

"It's actually where the phrase originated," she replied. "Vampires have been around a long time."

"I'm supposed to believe you were marking me for my protection, not claiming me as yours?"

A small smile crossed her lips and I shook my head.

"Perhaps…a little of both," she replied, her voice husky. "I chose you for the blade because you were the only one capable of wielding it."

I took a step back. "I'm sure my being immortal had *nothing* to do with that."

"Why do you find it difficult to comprehend I may have feelings for you?" she asked. "You do realize you are not the only immortal in existence?"

"True, but I'm the only one who can wield Ebonsoul," I answered. "Right?"

Her face darkened for a split second, and then she smiled again. I knew I was right. I also knew I was standing in front of one of the most efficient killing machines known to humankind.

"Your mage gave away something that wasn't his to give."

I knew what she meant. She was referring to *kokutan no ken,* the pair to the Ebonsoul. Ken, Chi's brother, had given the sword to Monty to keep safe.

When it became too dangerous, Monty sent the sword to Hades to keep it out of the wrong hands, thinking that would be the safest place to hide a weapon of that power level. What no one expected was for Hades to give the sword to the last Night Warden—Grey.

Now the Night Warden had bonded to the sword, which meant the only way to get it back was to kill Grey, who also happened to be a dark mage. No one was getting that sword back anytime soon.

"Monty didn't give it away, he placed it somewhere safe."

"That sword was the check and balance within the Dark Council," she said. "And it is now being wielded by the Night Warden."

It was my turn to smile. "The sword, really? We both know the real check and balance within the Dark Council is you."

"The sword was able to—" she began.

"The sword was just a symbol, but it meant nothing if you weren't holding it."

Chi looked away for a moment. "The creature behind the Lucent, the one that attacked the hound of

Hades…"

"Tartarus?"

For a moment I almost said tartarsauce, but Chi didn't have Monty's tolerant sense of humor. My trying to make fun of Tartar Boy could get me violently impaled.

Chi nodded. "He has been in motion for some time now. Always behind the scenes, always hidden, pulling the strings."

"Taking Persephone and Hades doesn't seem very behind the scenes to me," I said. "You think he's making a move?"

"He has been 'making a move,' as you call it, for longer than we've both been alive. These beings give new meaning to the term 'long game'."

"What does he want, do you know?"

"My sources tell me that he wants Hades."

"He already has Hades, what more does he want?"

"Not Hades, the god," she said, her voice dark. "Hades, the domain."

I remained silent for a few seconds. Why would Tartarus want Hades?

"He can't just take a domain, can he?" I asked. "Besides, he has his own domain to deal with. Why would he want Hades?"

"This being, Tartarus, is powerful," she said. "Stronger than all of the Olympians combined. If he wants this domain, it must contain something of interest."

"We can't let him have Hades—the god or the place."

She narrowed her eyes at me. "Simon, you do not

possess the power to stop this being, not even with your mage and"— she raised an eyebrow and looked down at Peaches—"your Hellhound."

"What is the Dark Council going to do?" I asked. "Are you just going to let them get away with taking Hades and Persephone?"

"Our concern is securing the Underworld," Chi answered, her voice cold. "We do not meddle in the affairs of gods. We deal with immediate threats and neutralize them."

"Basically, you're saying the Dark Council can't or won't move against Tartarus. He's too strong."

"He's too strong for us, and for you," she said, pointing at my chest. "Stay away from this one, Simon. We have a plan to close off the Underworld and seal it, denying this Tartarus entry into our world."

"What happened to the whole 'filling in the void left by Hades' and dealing with warring factions?" I demanded, letting my anger rise. Not exactly a wise choice, but I hated how bureaucracies operated. The Dark Council was just a supernatural organization of red tape.

"The Council will fill in the void, and we will put down any faction that rises," Chi answered, with an edge to match mine. "Our purpose is to prevent another supernatural war."

"By increasing the Dark Council's power base?" I asked.

"By any means necessary," she said, giving me a hard stare.

"Won't be too hard to secure the Underworld if Hades is missing. Have you wondered what his brothers might say about this?"

"I shouldn't be telling you this," she said, placing a hand on my arm, "but several pantheons are in accord with this plan. Including the Olympians."

"In accord?" I said, momentarily confused. A picture was forming, and I wasn't liking the image. "The Valkyrie? Odin and the Norse are in on this too?"

"They felt Hades and his Underworld were too dangerous to leave uncontrolled without some kind of oversight," Chi answered slowly. "It would be best to secure the Underworld, and then form a cross-pantheon task force to deal with Tartarus."

"And Hades?" I asked, brushing her hand off my arm. I was angry and apparently willing to risk my life. "You're going to steal his home, and what—stick him in a cell? What about Persephone?"

"They will both be well taken care of," she replied, her voice arctic. "The Olympians assure us they will be relocated and kept safe."

"Are you insane? You can't *trust* gods. This whole plan is crazy. How did the Dark Council buy into this—wait, what does the Council get out of this?"

"The safety of the city and the prevention of another supernatural war," Chi answered, lying to my face. "That is our only concern."

"What do the other pantheons get?" I asked. "What do the Norse and Olympians get? They don't care about supernatural wars. Hell, Odin is preparing for the war of all wars. Ragnarok isn't going to be a skirmish. It's supposed to be the end of the world as they know it."

"Walk away from this while you still can. No one in

the Council will give you special consideration if you interfere in what we are trying to achieve."

"Are you threatening me?"

"I'm warning you," Chi replied, "the only one you're going to receive. This is beyond you and your mage. It's even beyond me."

"But not beyond the Dark Council," I said. "Who made the call? Who thought this clusterfuck was a good idea?"

"That's irrelevant," she said. "All you need to know is the entire Dark Council will be mobilized for this. Mages, Vampires, and Weres."

"Clearly you aren't the one leading the Dark Council in this plan," I answered. "Did Erik think this was a good idea?"

"Stay away from this, Simon. You may be cursed alive, but pursuing this will get you killed—permanently."

"Got it," I said, my voice hard. "You do what you have to do, and I'll do the same."

She shook her head slowly. "I have to return to the Council and inform them of this new development," Chi said. "Our mages are already working on an Underworld seal. For once, listen to the voice of reason and keep out of this."

"I barely listen to the voice inside my head that usually tells me to run the other way, and now you want me to listen to the voice of reason?" I said. "Why would I start setting precedents now? Besides, I doubt Monty is going to leave this one alone."

"About that…" Chi said. "The Dark Council is considering taking action against your mage."

"Taking action?" I asked. "What exactly does that mean?"

Chi looked off into the distance. "Your mage is gradually stepping into darkness," she said quietly. "Even now, his sorceress is trying to stop him from pursuing Hades."

I remembered how easily Monty used blood magic. Chi was right. It was getting easier for him to use unstable and dangerous spells. This didn't mean the Dark Council had the right to 'take action,' though, whatever that meant.

"I'm going to say this once," I said, letting the anger lace my words. "If the Council moves against Monty, they move against me."

"You know I speak the truth. Even earlier this evening he used blood magic," Chi said gently. "His Golden Circle may not see that as an infraction, but the Dark Council does."

"What are they going to do?"

"When a mage goes dark, the mages of the Dark Council evaluate the reasons, the context, and the frequency."

"Any time Monty has used a dark spell, it's been to save this city," I said. "He's not a dark mage and isn't a threat."

"Two void vortices within the city, in addition to several important structures and buildings destroyed or obliterated by his actions," she replied. "Not to mention his presence has cost the life of several NYTF officers and personnel. Here and abroad."

"What are you saying?"

"Would you like me to give you the tally for your

little trip to London?" she asked. "The only reason we aren't facing an international incident is because several of the older mages and the Dark Council made reparations."

"There were extenuating—"

"No," Chi said, holding up a finger as her glare cut through me. "You summoned an unsanctioned water elemental in the Thames and destroyed part of the Tower of London."

"If we hadn't," I started, "London would be a crater right now. You were there, you know this. We saved lives."

"But you can't seem to do this without massive destruction," Chi said, keeping her voice controlled. "You save lives, yes, but then you go and destroy landmarks. Structures that people treasure."

"Are you saying buildings are more important than human lives?"

"These aren't just buildings," she said with a shake of her head. "You are obliterating parts of history. A history that many feel is special."

"The water elemental wanted to help," I said, looking at Peaches. "He saved Peaches. We barely damaged the Tower of London."

"It's enough to say that you damaged the *Tower of London.* You have no clue how many in the Penumbra Consortium wanted you both executed, along with your helldog."

"Monty isn't dangerous. Neither is Peaches."

"The mage is a threat, and once this Hades situation is dealt with, the Dark Council will move to exile, erase, or incarcerate him."

"And Peaches?"

"They will try to euthanize your creature," she said softly. "He singlehandedly destroyed the Tate Modern. The Penumbra Consortium especially dislikes him."

"You realize he's not a regular dog?" I asked. "If they even look at Peaches sideways, I'll *erase* them."

"He's almost as destructive as the mage," Chi replied, looking at Peaches, who gave her a low rumble. "I'm sorry. They feel he's too dangerous to leave alive."

"The only ones who will be sorry will be the ones who come at us," I said, barely keeping my rage under control. "The Dark Council is declaring war against us?"

"It's for the greater good of the city."

"Bullshit, and you know it," I said. "We've saved this city several times—both Peaches and Monty."

"Their *presence* in the city is the threat," Chi said. "*They* are the reason the city has needed saving. You've said it yourself, your mage and the helldog are the reason you get blamed all the time."

She was right, but I wasn't going to let the Dark Council lay a finger on Monty or Peaches—not without a fight.

"Like I said before, you do what you have to do, and I'll do the same," I answered quietly. "No one is going to exile or incarcerate them while I'm still breathing."

"He cast a blood rune tonight," Chi said. "Did you know that was forbidden by the Dark Council and the Golden Circle?"

"I do now," I said. "We were in danger of being melted, along with an entire building."

"When aren't you in danger?"

It was actually a good question.

"The Lucent were going to melt the building and everyone inside of it," I replied, reining in my anger. "You wanted us to what? Just let it happen?"

"It's always something cataclysmic with you two—excuse me, three," she snapped, waving my words away. "Tonight it was a blood rune. What's next, a blood sacrifice? Is he going to summon a golem and destroy your enemies?"

"That's a little dark, even for Monty."

"He's changing, Simon. The sooner you realize this, the sooner you can help him," Chi said. "Roxanne, I can understand. She loves him. But you need to see this situation clearly. He's dangerous."

"Monty would never go dark. It's not who he is."

"You have to make a choice, Simon," Chi said, her voice suddenly soft. "Choose well."

I turned when I heard Roxanne's voice. When I turned back, Chi was gone.

NINETEEN

ROXANNE AND MONTY headed our way. She looked angry and he looked like someone had spiked his tea with old coffee. Whatever conversation they'd just had hadn't ended on a positive note.

"I will be keeping Corbel here for observation," Roxanne said, looking at Peaches and rubbing him behind the ears. "I'm also going to need to run some tests on Hellhound saliva. Apparently, it has incredible healing properties. Who knew?"

<I knew.>

<I know you did.>

<My saliva has incredible healing properties, but not as amazing as the beautiful Rags. Her saliva is the best.>

<I don't think she sees you the same way you see her. She seems a bit preoccupied with Cece.>

<That only means she is focused on her work. It's not easy keeping a human out of trouble. I should know.>

<You should know? What does that mean?>

"Is Corbel conscious?" Monty asked, looking into the room. "I need to have a word."

Roxanne nodded. "He should be able to answer some questions, but do not tax him, Tristan. He's in no condition to exert himself. Hound of Hades or not, he needs rest."

"Simon, I'll meet you back at the car," Monty said, pressing on the door and giving Roxanne a look. "We'll continue our conversation later, if you have time."

"I'd like that, Tristan. Over tea perhaps?"

"Perfect," he said, stepping to the side and entering Corbel's room. He glanced back and gave me a look in Montyspeak that said, 'brace yourself for the wrath of the angry sorceress.' I wasn't looking forward to that.

"I need to do some rounds," Roxanne said, grabbing a clipboard. "Walk with me, Simon."

"What about Peaches? Isn't he going to scare the personnel?"

"Not in this wing. Besides, he's registered with Haven as your service dog," she answered. "He can go anywhere in the facility."

"My Hellhound has more clearance than I do?"

"*His* saliva probably saved Corbel's life," Roxanne snapped. "What can *your* saliva do, besides keep your mouth moist?"

Ouch. It was clear she wasn't happy. It was a good thing I'd saved my Sting impersonation for another day. She'd probably blast me after the first note. Not everyone could appreciate my vocal stylings. It took a very refined ear, not that I was going to share that with the angry sorceress.

"It certainly doesn't have healing properties," I said as we entered an empty room. "Who's in here, the invisible—?"

"Simon, what are you doing?" Roxanne asked with an edge to her voice. She turned, locking her eyes with mine. "Don't you care about him?"

The questions caught me off guard for a split second.

"Are we still referring to Peaches?"

"Peaches? Are you daft? What is wrong with you?"

"Those sound like loaded questions."

"I'm seriously considering admitting the both of you into the mental ward until this Hades thing is over."

Her voice went up a few decibels and simultaneously dropped into menacing territory, setting off all my danger alarms. An angry sorceress is a fearsome sight.

I raised my hands in surrender, stepped back, and made sure I had access to my weapons. Monty would be pissed if I shot his…I don't know what he called Roxanne, but I know he didn't want me shooting or stabbing her. Aside from her intense gaze, black energy had formed around her hands.

"Roxanne, is there a reason your hands are covered in black energy?" I asked carefully. "Maybe you can tell me which 'him' I'm supposed to care about specifically?"

She looked down suddenly and gasped. "I'm sorry," she answered, momentarily flustered. "I'm exhausted and I've been working doubles."

She shook her hands and the black energy vanished.

"Chi told you, didn't she?"

Roxanne nodded. "The Dark Council will target Tristan as soon as whatever is going on with Hades is resolved."

"Did she tell you what she meant by *resolved*?"

"What does it matter? Hades is a god. He can take care of himself," Roxanne answered. "You're Tristan's shieldbearer, Simon. You have a responsibility to *him*."

"It matters because it's wrong," I said. "He may be a god, but they're setting him up, stealing his home. For some artifacts?"

"Do you think Hades is blameless in this? Are you under some notion that he's 'good' and 'just'?"

"I know he isn't," I said, looking down at my Hellhound. The Hellhound Hades had given me. The same Hellhound that had saved Monty and me more than once. "We all have a dark side, some darker than most. Doesn't mean we let them do what they want just because they can."

Roxanne nodded. "I knew you'd say that," she answered, shaking her head. "After Tristan's last shift, the mages of the Dark Council pose little threat to him, individually."

"But together?"

"They can and will overwhelm him. You must find a way to neutralize the Dark Council mages before they attack."

"Our schedule is a little full at the moment," I said. "You know, gods of the Underworld to locate? Three Lucent to stop, and a scary Tartar being to thwart?"

"It's not just the Dark Council you need to worry about," Roxanne said, her face grim. "There are other mages."

"Other mages?"

"Dark mages who would destroy the Council and would want nothing more than to have Tristan on their side," she said. "You can't let him succumb to the dark magic."

"This is Monty," I said. "He would never go da—"

"He used blood magic tonight," she said. "Blood magic is dangerous, unstable, and makes him vulnerable to darker magic. You must not let him use blood magic again."

"You want *me* to stop *him* from using blood magic? How exactly am I supposed to do this?"

"You know a spell, yes? A magic missile?"

I heard the words, but my brain couldn't process them.

"You want me to shoot Monty with a magic missile?"

"If you see him attempting to use blood magic again, yes," she said, crossing her arms and setting her jaw. "Being his shieldbearer means your job is to protect him, even when that means protecting him from himself."

"Are we talking about the same Monty?" I asked. "Can you stop him from doing anything?"

She grabbed my right hand and traced a rune on my palm. The symbol flared black and red for a few seconds before disappearing.

"What was that? Was that—?"

"No," she said and stared at me. "It's not blood or dark magic. Being a sorceress doesn't automatically mean dark magic, you know."

"Sorry, I've never encountered a good sorceress," I said. "And your rep is not a good one."

"I could say the same thing about immortal detectives with Hellhound companions."

"Good point," I answered. "What does this symbol do?"

I looked at my hand. The area where she had traced the rune pulsed with power. I couldn't see the symbol, but I could feel the power racing through my body.

"That will help strengthen your spell until you grow in power on your own," she said. "You will have to use that hand to fire the spell or it won't be enhanced."

"So this *isn't* blood magic," I said, holding up my hand and expecting it to burst into flames at any second. "Just making sure."

"Blood magic is forbidden, even amongst practitioners of dark magic. Do you know why?"

"It uses the lifeforce of the caster," I said. "Prolonged use can kill the magic-user."

"Almost," she said. "It uses the lifeforce of the caster, and allows the psyche to be twisted and corrupted into something else... something evil. A mage of Tristan's level becoming dark would be nearly unstoppable."

"That's why they want to erase him? Because he *may* become dark? After all he's done to save this city?"

"Don't be naïve, Simon," she replied. "The fact that he's not part of the Council means they can't control him."

"If they can't control him, it means he's a threat."

"A formidable one," she answered. "One they need to neutralize."

"If they move against him, they have to deal with me."

"Chi risked everything by telling you their plans," Roxanne answered. "But make no mistake, they will come after Tristan. If you stand in their way, they will try to eliminate you as well."

"I'd like to see them try."

TWENTY

I WAITED FOR Monty in the Dark Goat.

Peaches sprawled in the back, taking up the entire seat. I glanced back at him through the rear-view mirror. Why had Hades given him to me? Was this part of some deeper plan, or did he really want me to bond with him?

No matter what the motivation was, I couldn't imagine my life without him, and there was no way I was going to let someone try and hurt him. Part of me wanted to let them try, just so he could go Peaches XL on them.

<*The angry man didn't make my sausage. Did you ask?*>

<*I'm sorry, boy. I'll ask as soon as he gets here. He's been a little busy.*>

<*Busy? You can never be too busy for meat.*>

<*I agree. Would you like me to try and make you some sausage?*>

<*Are we under attack? Are bad men coming?*>

<*No, why do you ask?*>

<*You want to make me sausage. The only reason you want to*

do that is so I can make explosive bad air.>

<*No, I was just thinking if you didn't want to—never mind, let's wait for Monty.*>

<*I think that is safer. Your last sausage broke my stomach. If you lick me, would I get better?*>

<*I don't think so, boy. All you would be is sick and slobbery.*>

<*That doesn't sound as good as meat. I'll wait for the angry man. Maybe you should practice?*>

<*Last time I made you a sausage, I was practicing.*>

<*Your practice needs practice.*>

At some point without my realizing it, my Hellhound had become a Zen Meat Master.

Monty got into the car a few seconds later. He looked like he needed a large cup of Earl Grey.

"Is it tea time yet?" I asked, turning on the Dark Goat. "You look like a 'spot of tea will do nicely'," I said in my best Julia Child voice. "Either that, or I can lend you my flask?"

"It's always tea time," Monty said with a nod. "We need to see James."

"The Randy Rump?" I asked. "Isn't that a little far just for tea? Are you sure you don't want my flask?"

"Randy Rump will suffice, thank you," he said. "I think you should keep your imbibing from that flask to a minimum. It's covered in glowing skulls and was given to you by Hel. I doubt it meets any nutritional requirements."

"It's javambrosia, Monty," I said reverently. "It's like getting punched in the face—by an angel. Are you serious, you want the Rump?"

"The portal that was used against Hades was not a

typical teleportation circle. I can't open a doorway there."

"Where is 'there' exactly?"

"Tartarus," Monty answered. "There is a good chance Hades and Persephone now reside in Tartarus. We need a gate to access that domain."

"Chi said something about sealing Tartarus away from the Underworld," I said. "Is that what she meant? Sealing this gate?"

"The probability of sealing Tartarus, the entity, is miniscule," Monty said, slowly shaking his head. "His power is staggering. Sealing the domain, however, though monumentally difficult, is more likely. Our best bet is sealing the gate."

"How many of these gates are there?"

"Two," Monty answered. "Well, one now. One gate was located in Hades' office."

"In…the office?" I asked. "The office that no longer exists?"

"Yes, clearly *that* gate is no longer an option."

"What happened to the other one?"

"Corbel informs me no one knew about the gates."

"He knew, Hades knew, and I'm going to guess Persephone knew," I said, pumping the brakes before I rear-ended a Prius into its component parts.

"Its existence was not common knowledge."

"Who would create and install a gate like that?" I asked. "Someone besides those three had the information."

"True, Hades indicated as much with the soulkeeper." Monty rubbed his chin in thought. "Someone in his inner circle betrayed him."

"We need to find out how large that circle is," I said. "Do these gates shift out of existence? Do we know how they're made?"

"According to Corbel, Hades personally oversaw their construction," Monty said. "He anticipated an incursion at some point."

"This gate," I started, "was it like a teleportation circle, one way and one location only, or could it go anywhere?"

"Gates of this type," Monty began, "if it's the one I have in mind, can be used to travel to any location, providing the proper runic sequence is known."

"And they operate both ways?"

"Yes, they facilitate travel back and forth."

"Hades had a feeling Tartarsauce was going to move against him? Must've been a reason for that. Someone thought that gate was a threat."

"Indeed, considering it's been obliterated."

"And the second gate?"

"Beneath the newest neutral location in the city, hidden in plain sight, as it were."

"There's a gate to Tartarus in the Randy Rump?"

"Not *in* the Randy Rump," Monty said. "*Under* it."

"Jimmy's going to love that." I shook my head. "I'm going to let you explain that one to him."

"We will be using an alternate entrance to access the gate," Monty said. "Letting James, or anyone, know about the existence of the second gate would put their lives in danger. The Randy Rump would be blasted into oblivion."

"That was the reason for the building demolition," I said, making the connection. "The Lucent knew about the gate in Hades' office and were instructed to shut it down."

"An accurate assessment."

"And here I thought it was because you gave off that patented Montague cheerfulness."

"Droll, as usual," Monty replied. "The Lucent were ensuring no one could access Tartarus."

"How difficult is it to create one of these gates?"

"It requires a high-level mastery of temporal and spatial manipulation," Monty replied. "The cost and construction is prohibitive."

"Where did they build it?"

"The second gate was constructed in secret," Monty said. "When the Randy Rump was destroyed by Beck, a specific construction company was responsible for the rebuilding."

"Let me guess, Terra Sur Global?"

"The one and the same," Monty said. "Seems Hades planned for this contingency and only told one person."

"Corbel," I said. "Means he's not our inside man. If he were, the Rump would be a crater right now."

The Randy Rump was a block away from the Moscow and it stayed open all night, only closing for a few hours in the early morning. It catered to the early evening and nighttime clientele—which was most of the supernatural community.

The Rump had also become a popular meeting place since the Dark Council had declared its neutral status. It had gone from "butcher shop" to "butcher shop, restaurant, and meeting hall" in a few short weeks.

We were about twenty minutes away at this hour with light traffic. "Jimmy probably has your Earl Grey stocked by now," I said, swerving around two NYC taxis that were intent on cutting me off. Driving in NYC was the equivalent of being in a demolition derby where you were the target car. "What was that name again? Blarney & Sons?"

"Harney & Sons, Victorian London Fog. They have a special factory in Yorkshire," Monty said, rubbing his temple. "James assured me he was importing directly from them."

"You really should just switch to Death Wish," I said. "It's the closest thing to drinking divinity."

"Does Death Wish make tea?"

"That sentence alone is sacrilege, Monty," I said, shaking my head. "Are you trying to anger the java gods? Caffeina will not be mocked."

"Caffeina, seriously?" Monty asked with a short glare. "Were you exposed to some brain debilitating illness at Haven?"

"Don't anger her," I said. "If you anger her, she'll turn your tea or coffee to water—lukewarm, horrible-tasting water. I suggest you not discuss coffee—ever."

"My sentiments exactly when you discuss tea," he said, resting his head back and closing his eyes. "Let's refrain from discussing gods or goddesses, real or imagined, until I have my tea."

"We have a problem."

"You mean other than the god of the Underworld and his wife being abducted, and the three beings of near godlike power roaming this plane, controlled by a primordial entity bent on stealing a domain that isn't his?"

"Yes, the Dark Council thinks you're going dark."

"You realize we have more pressing matters than what the Dark Council thinks?"

"They want to erase you, followed by exile or incarceration," I said, letting the words hang in the air. "I'm serious."

"Your vampire told you this?"

I nodded. "Just to be safe, let me ask—do you feel sudden anger or irritation?"

"As soon as you started asking this line of questioning."

"How about wardrobe? Do you feel like trading in the suits for something with a hood? Preferably in black?"

"No. Are you mad?" he asked. "Something with a hood?"

"How about cackling?" I asked. "Any sudden urge to laugh maniacally? Extend your fingers. Do you feel like unleashing lightning?"

"The only urge I'm feeling is unleashing a flame orb at you."

"Okay, last one," I said. "Repeat after me: only now at the end, do you understand."

"Absolutely not," Monty answered. "The only thing I understand is how pointless these questions are."

"Well, I think it's safe to say you haven't gone dark—yet."

"I'm a Montague. Montagues do *not* go dark."

"I'd say your Uncle Dex is on the fringe there," I said. "I mean the Morrigan? Really?"

"My uncle isn't dark, he's insane. There's a difference."

"True," I agreed and grew serious. "The Dark

Council is coming for you right after this Hades thing is dealt with. They aren't kidding."

"And you?" Monty asked, looking at me. "What do you think?"

"I think all mages are a little touched," I answered. "Montagues more than most. But, no, I don't think you're going dark."

"I'm not," Monty said. "Nor do I have any desire to have an angry sorceress hunt me down, and I quote 'introduce me to such pain the likes of which humanity has never seen its equal' before ending me."

"That sounds like Roxanne," I said. "Can you avoid using the blood spells?"

If he said 'no' or gave me the addicts excuse—'I have it under control or I can stop whenever I want to', I would have to be careful. It would mean that despite the denials there was a real risk of his becoming dark.

"The blood rune was necessary," Monty said. "It was the only way to stop that spell from the Lucent."

"Was it the *only* way?"

"What are you getting at, Simon?" he asked defensively. "I'm the mage. If I tell you it was the only way, it was the *only* way."

I didn't like his tone, but I needed to push. I needed to make sure I wasn't losing him to the dark side.

"You're right," I said. "I'm not a mage. I'm just noticing that you're using these scarier spells more often. Two void vortices in the city, at The Eldorado you set the runes to go entropic, and in Hades' place you used a forbidden blood rune. To a non-mage, those spells look pretty dark."

"I understand," he said with a sigh. "In the future,

when our lives—along with those of countless innocents—are on the line, would you like me to consult with you about the darkness of the spell I'm about to cast, or should I just prevent death and devastation?"

"Let's prevent the death and devastation, thank you."

Monty nodded and pinched the bridge of his nose. "There is an axiom all mages learn early in their studies," he said, looking out the window. "Spells in the abstract are not good or bad, dark or light."

"Just depends on who's doing the casting?"

He nodded.

"Magic, energy, and the countless other names it's been given over the centuries is an amoral source of power," he replied. "The same spell I use to cast a teleportation circle can be used to move you from one place to another, or slice you in half."

"That's not very comforting," I said, turning on to 11th Avenue and heading downtown. "Just for the record, I'd like to be teleported in one piece, thank you."

"I'm just clarifying," he replied. "There are no 'scary' or 'evil' spells."

I slammed on the brakes, causing the Dark Goat to skid sideways for several feet before coming to a stop.

"I got it," I said. "It's not the spells that are evil or scary, just the people who wield them. Right?"

"Why did you stop suddenly?" Monty asked. "What's wrong?"

I pointed out of the passenger-side window. In the center of 11th Avenue, surrounded by a black nimbus of energy, stood Alnit the First.

"I think he qualifies for evil *and* scary."

"Bloody hell," Monty said under his breath. "We're sitting in a coffin. We need to get out."

"Won't the runes Cecil used protect the Dark Goat?"

"You don't understand," Monty said and started gesturing. The runes materialized and then flickered, disappearing. "The Lucent are older than the runes Cecil used. There's a good chance this Goat will end up like the first one."

"Oh c'mon," I said. "We just got this one. I really like the Dark Goat. Can't you just fire a Walnut remover at him?"

"Tristan Montague, Mage of the Golden Circle," Alnit said, his voice carrying over clearly despite the distance.

"This message is definitely for you," I said, opening the door and getting out, making sure to keep the Dark Goat between Alnit and me.

"Simon Strong, chosen of Kali, and bondmate to Peaches the Hellhound," Alnit continued. "My master wishes to commend you on invoking his attention."

"Well, shit," I said. "At least he got Peaches' name right."

"Indeed," Monty said. "Looks like it's a group message."

I stared at him. "Was that humor?"

"I have no idea what you're referring to," Monty deadpanned. "This situation is quite serious. Levity would be unbecoming in this moment."

"Right, Mr. Spock," I said, shaking my head as I opened the suicide door and let Peaches out. "We're about to get disintegrated but we should mind our decorum."

"Precisely," Monty answered, moving to my side of the Dark Goat. "The energy around him is unstable. If it impacts the runes of this vehicle—"

"Ground zero?" I asked.

"More or less. Emphasis on less—of everything. Starting with us."

<*Can I bite the bad man? I'm really hungry.*>

<*Do not bite the bad man. I'll take you to the place and get you twice as much meat. Just stay away from the bad man.*>

<*More than that. You promised and didn't ask the angry man for meat. Now I'm hungry.*>

I looked down at my voracious, bottomless Hellhound.

<*Are you serious? What do you mean more?*>

<*Yes. More than twice the meat. You promised. Or, I can just bite the bad man's leg off.*>

<*I didn't promise more than—fine. Just stay back. The black cloud around the bad man is dangerous.*>

<*See? Frank calls that upping the ants. Now, I get more meat.*>

<*It's 'upping the ante,' and I'm serious, no more talking to that lizard.*>

<*He's a dragon.*>

<*A menace is what he is.*>

"Wait a second," I said, raising a hand. "No one is *invoking* anything. Tell him, Monty."

"Who is your master, Lucent?" Monty asked, backing up. "Or do you fear speaking his name?"

"Fear?" Alnit said as the nimbus of energy increased around him. "You have no concept of the word, mage, but you will."

"Monty, can we not antagonize the Walnut?" I said under my breath. "He looks really eager to deliver his message, and it looks painful."

"My master is," said Alnit, "the Lord of the Abyss, the One who was before, the Keeper of the creatures of nightmares, the First Lightbringer, the immortal Tartarus, third of the Protogenoi."

"That's some resume. You tell Tartarsauce that we're flattered, really," I said, aware that the nimbus was still growing. "But we don't really need his attention. I'm sure he's busy elsewhere with his hostile takeovers and such. All we need is for him to return Hades and Mrs. Hades and we're good."

"You dare to command Tartarus?" Alnit asked, clearly offended. "You will suffer for your insolence, you impudent human."

"Can we say fragile egos?"

"That energy around him is acting as a null field," Monty said under his breath. "I can't cast."

"Which means?"

"Run."

TWENTY-ONE

BY THE TIME we stopped, we were a few hundred feet away from the psycho Walnut. He was still moving his arms and the energy signature I sensed from his direction felt angry and malevolent.

"That cloud around him is bad news," I said. "It feels evil."

"The cloud isn't evil," Monty said, his jaw set. "Its purpose is to neutralize everything around it. The Lucent controlling the cloud…*he* is one bloody evil bastard."

"So, what I'm sensing is his intent?"

"I'd say that intent is decidedly negative at this moment."

It took a moment to register what was happening. The black cloud of energy around Alnit seemed to slow down. The swirling mass around him almost froze in place as he smiled at us.

"I will enjoy ending your insignificant lives," Alnit said, his voice carrying over to us. He began moving his hands and the cloud around him coalesced.

It was the self-satisfied smile of superiority that always pissed me off. Especially when displayed by powerful creatures who think they're going to erase you from existence.

"I'm going to guess entropy rounds will be useless against that?" I said, backing up and still keeping the Dark Goat between the Lucent and me.

"About as effective as they were against him," Monty answered as he traced runes in the air. "We need to use the vehicle to slow it down."

"I thought you said you couldn't cast?"

"I said I couldn't cast *near* that energy field around him," Monty corrected. "With enough distance, the effect of the null field is diminished."

"You don't have a Walnut-cracking spell in your arsenal, do you?" I asked, looking down 11th Avenue at Alnit. "He's going to kill the Dark Goat, Monty. I'm not happy."

"I'm afraid it can't be helped, but we can take solace in knowing that Cecil will now have a method to destroy the Beast."

"That gives me no solace," I said. "Can't you throw a shield around it?"

"Tartarus wishes you to know," Alnit said, gesturing, "that it will be an honor for you to perish, understanding that the mighty and fearsome Tartarus gave your pitiful existence momentary consideration."

"I like this Tartarsauce less and less every second," I said, angry at the thought of losing another Goat. "Monty, tell me you have a plan. One that involves shredding this Walnut."

"I do, but I don't think you're going to like it."

"Can we save the Dark Goat?"

"Unlikely."

"Shit, does it involve blood magic?"

"Yes, your blade, and your creature as well."

"Do we get to pound the Walnut?"

"Repeatedly," Monty said, gesturing and forming several shields around us. "Are you ready?"

"Does it matter?" I said, unsheathing Ebonsoul.

"Yes, it does," he answered. "He's a Lucent. We can't afford to take him lightly."

"I understand. Tell me the plan."

I looked at Monty after he was done sharing what he wanted to do. For the first time, I not only questioned his sanity, but mine for agreeing to go through with his idea.

Alnit extended an arm and unleashed the nimbus of black energy at us. I didn't have to look at him to know that it was advancing on us—fast.

Monty cast another series of shields wide enough to cover the street. We were behind a semi-circle of concentric shields.

"When that energy hits the Dark Goat, it will cause an explosion," Monty said. "That will be our signal to move."

"You want Peaches and me to race *forward* into the explosion?"

"Yes, once the blast reaches the last set of shields, you advance," Monty said. "Go through the debris of the Dark Goat and straight at the Lucent."

"Where we split up, Peaches pounces, and I introduce him to Ebonsoul while you blast him."

"Exactly," Monty said as dark violet energy covered

his arms. "With a little luck, we'll be able to 'crack this Walnut,' as you say."

"We're insane," I said as the black energy crashed into the Dark Goat and exploded.

TWENTY-TWO

THE RUNES COVERING the Dark Goat burst with bright orange light as the car exploded into its component parts. Time slowed as the car expanded into smaller pieces. For a brief moment, I saw an exploded view of my beloved Dark Goat.

The irony wasn't lost on me.

"Now, Simon." Monty's voice sounded distant, as sound and pressure reacted to the black cloud, interacting with the ancient runes of the Dark Goat. "It's at the last shield."

I raced forward with Peaches next to me. That's when I felt the first shift of energy. The parts of the Dark Goat that were expanding outward a second earlier remained frozen in space.

Peaches and I ran through the expanded Dark Goat. I noticed the violet runes pulsing as the pieces began moving backward and the Dark Goat started reassembling.

"Stupid fool," Alnit said, drawing his guns. "You race to your death."

<Can I bite him now?>

<You can go bite him now, boy. Just don't chew. He's probably infected with something gross.>

<Like your healthy meat?>

<Worse. Bite and rip off an arm or a leg, but no chewing.>

Peaches blinked out a second later as I threw Ebonsoul. I aimed high for Alnit's chest. He fired several times in my direction, but I was ready with my own shield.

The rounds didn't shatter my shield, but the impact launched me to the side and nearly broke my arm. I rolled for several feet when I felt another shift. I jumped to my feet with a wince and drew Grim Whisper as my body flushed hot, dealing with the pain and damage.

Peaches reappeared around Alnit's left leg. His jaws locked on his thigh. The momentary distraction of a Hellhound clamping down on his leg broke Alnit's guard long enough to allow Ebonsoul to puncture his chest.

A rush of power filled me as Ebonsoul siphoned energy from Alnit. The look of surprise on his face was soon transformed by rage.

Alnit aimed a gun at Peaches. I aimed Grim Whisper and fired several times. He blocked my rounds with his forearm blade. By the time he looked down, Peaches had vanished. I jumped behind the reassembled Dark Goat as he opened fire again.

I patted her side, giving Cecil thanks for whatever insane runes he used to keep her intact, and looked up in time to see a black basketball-sized orb race past me toward Alnit.

"Monty, what the hell was that?"

"Get in the car, now," Monty said, his voice grim. He was breathing hard and his face was paler than usual.

"I truly hope it's still operational," Monty said, out of breath. "Can you start it?"

"I'm still wondering how it put itself back together," I said. "What kind of runes did Cecil use on this thing?"

"Would take too long to explain," Monty said, looking over the hood. "Once that orb reaches him, we need to be elsewhere. Where is your creat—?"

Peaches reappeared next to me. I opened the suicide door and shoved him in. Monty was already inside by the time I got behind the wheel.

"What did you launch at him?" I asked, not liking the fact that he kept looking in Alnit's direction. "It felt like the building-melter, only concentrated."

"That was an anti-spell," he said, his voice clipped. "Keyed specifically to Alnit's energy signature."

"How did you manage that?" I asked, feeling the energy siphon from Ebonsoul. The intensity of the power threatened to blind me. My head felt like it was being squeezed in a vise. "What is your spell doing?"

"No time…drive or die," he said with a gasp. "We need distance. That orb is unstable. Retrieve your blade before its's too late."

I pressed my hand to the dashboard, starting the engine with a roar. I extended my other arm out of the Dark Goat and opened my hand. A silver mist formed around it, coalescing into Ebonsoul a second later. I sheathed my blade with a grunt. It wanted me to continue the process of absorption, and resisted taking solid form.

"An anti-spell? What the hell is an—?"

"Bloody hell, Simon. Drive!"

I stepped on the gas, and the Dark Goat lurched forward. We raced downtown and away from Alnit, who was the epicenter of whatever nastiness Monty had launched at him.

"Didn't you hear what I said?" Monty asked, looking out of the window. "We need distance *away* from the Lucent."

The Dark Goat wasn't moving. The engine roared and I could feel it wanting to leap forward, but something held it in place.

"Pedal is on the floor," I snapped back. "Either the Walnut has a tractor beam, or that orb you launched is more unstable than you thought."

We were losing ground, as the Dark Goat slowly slid back toward Alnit and destruction. It was at this point that I realized just how insane the Montague mages were. Monty opened the door and stepped out.

"What the hell are you doing?" I asked. "You plan on convincing him to let the orb take him out?"

"In a manner of speaking," Monty answered. "I'm cutting the tether. Get ready to drive."

Monty bowed his head and placed his hands together in prayer position, which I thought was an excellent idea since I was fresh out of them.

I saw his mouth moving but heard nothing, as interlacing red circles formed between his now outstretched hands. He brought his hands close to his face, and for a moment it appeared as if he were whispering to the circles. I recognized them from the lobby of the Terra Sur Global. They were oblivion circles.

In the distance, I heard Alnit laughing. Clearly the black orb of destruction wasn't working. Monty jumped back in the Dark Goat, closed the door, and strapped in. I saw the blood drip from a nostril as he grabbed a tissue to stop the flow.

"Did you send him the right orb of devastation?" I asked, looking behind us in the rear-view mirror. "Because that one sounds like the orb of hilarity."

"There's no such orb," Monty replied, glancing back. "The circles should catalyze the orb any second now."

"Those were oblivion circles."

"I know," Monty said. "I used the pattern from the building. They should be quite effective."

"Since when do you use oblivion circles?"

"Since the servant of a primordial entity is trying to kill us."

I nodded my head. "You are a scary mage, Monty."

"Get ready," he said, tightening his seat belt.

"Ready? Ready for what?"

"That."

A bass note sounded and punched me in the stomach. A second later, a crack of lightning followed by the roar of thunder filled the night.

The Dark Goat leaped forward as a column of black and red energy shot into the sky behind us.

"Drive or die?" I asked.

Monty nodded as we raced downtown, away from Alnit and oblivion.

TWENTY-THREE

"THAT SHOULD GET his attention," Monty said, closing his eyes as we raced downtown. "Head for the Rump. I need my tea."

I expected a call from Ramirez any second now, but I figured he was too busy with the newly renovated Terra Sur building to chew me a new one. Knowing Angel, he'd get around to it sooner rather than later.

"Do I want to know whose attention we're trying to get?"

"Tartarus," Monty said. "We need him to come to us."

"I thought we were going to use the gate, get Mr. and Mrs. Hades, seal it, and call it a job well done?"

"According to the texts, Tartarus—the place—is immense," Monty said. "We would get inexorably disoriented and could end up wandering the domain for centuries, possibly longer. No, we need him to come to us."

"And you think he's going to come to us because—?"

"We just eliminated one of his Lucent, something

that's not supposed to be possible."

"Are you sure Walnut is gone?" I asked, glancing in the rear-view. "This is the same guy who blocked entropy rounds—with his face."

"The spell I hit him with ensured he wasn't going to report back to his master," Monty said with the hint of a smile, turning my blood to ice. "His mistake was underestimating how much of a threat we posed."

"The threat was lethal," I said, looking at Monty. "Especially if you're a crazy mage and your last name is Montague."

"Tartarus is arrogant. He will see this as an affront. He will come to us."

"Why not just send the other Lucent after us?"

"We dispatched one. He knows we can do it again. No, I'm counting on his ego forcing his hand. There's something he seeks and we have to find out what that is. If he had it, Alnit wouldn't have tried to eliminate us tonight."

"For once I hope you're wrong. I'm not in a hurry to meet another primordial being. One was enough to last me several lifetimes."

"I agree," Monty said. "I don't think we have a choice."

I parked in front of the Randy Rump.

My phone buzzed as we got out of the Dark Goat and walked into the Rump. I looked at the number and for a few seconds, really considering sending it to voicemail.

It was Ramirez again. Sending him to voicemail was only preventing the inevitable. Sooner or later I'd have to hear all about how we destroyed Terra Sur Global. I opted for ripping the Band-Aid off fast and answered the call.

"Ramirez, that wasn't us downtown," I started. "We have some heavy hitters in town and—"

"Shut up, Strong," Ramirez answered, his voice low. "Can you make this line secure?"

"Hold on."

I pressed my index finger to the rear of my phone and waited for the Fort Knox icon to show up on my screen. The biometric reader was keyed to my fingerprint along with a retinal scanner.

The call paused for a few moments as it bounced across several sites, and then piggybacked on another line in a backhaul. From there, it jumped to a T3 line and rerouted the call, repeating the process several times. Hack had tried to explain it to me one time. All I got was that it made it impossible to trace the call.

"You there?" Ramirez asked after a few seconds. "Strong?"

"I'm on a Blueberry with quadcrypt," I answered. "Only way to make it more secure would be to speak in code."

Hack had repurposed smart phones and added several unsanctioned features for Monty and me. He happened to be one of the most dangerous cybercriminals I'd ever encountered. Every three-letter agency on the planet feared, admired, and hunted him.

Give Hack a computer and time, and nothing in the digital or real world was safe from his reach.

"That's good," Ramirez answered. "Your Hack friend sent me one of his phones. He said if I ever had an emergency and needed to talk to you, to only use this phone."

"Hack never told me he gave you a phone," I said. "Then again, it's hard to have a coherent conversation with him."

"No kidding," Ramirez answered. "I didn't understand half of what he was saying. Only to use this phone if I needed to call you with sensitive information."

Monty stepped into the Randy Rump while I stood outside. I knew he really needed his tea, and it was safer for the tri-state area if he got his cuppa sooner rather than later.

If Ramirez was calling me on a Hack phone, it was serious.

"I'm listening," I said, standing outside the Randy Rump and scanning the street. "Talk to me."

"Strong, I'm calling to give you a heads up," Ramirez started. "We have a history and you've always been solid. Usually a solid pain in my ass, but you and your wizard friend look out for the city when you aren't breaking it."

"Is this about downtown?"

"Forget downtown. You need to get out of the city."

"What? What's going on?"

"You should plan for a few days, or years."

"Who is it?"

"Dark Council. One of my sources inside says they're coming for you in the next few days."

"Next few days? Wait, you have sources *inside* the Dark Council?"

"Focus, Strong. They're coming. Not just for the wizard, but for you, and that thing you call a dog."

I didn't bother correcting him on Monty being a mage, but I drew a line at calling Peaches a dog.

"His name is Peaches. He's a Hellhound, not a dog."

I heard Ramirez sigh. "I don't care if his name is Apricots," he answered. "They're coming after you."

"Who are they sending?"

"DCE Wolves."

"Shit."

DCE were Dark Council Enforcers. They were supernatural police whose only purpose was to stop other supernaturals from breaking Dark Council law.

Organized in military units, each faction operated in squads, platoons, companies, and battalions. They were always led by senior Dark Council members.

"How many squads?" I asked, expecting at least one squad, maybe two. "I think we can avoid a squad until they calm down."

"They're only sending one," Ramirez said, his voice grim. "One battalion."

I pulled my phone away and stared at it for a few seconds in disbelief. A battalion was, at minimum, three hundred DCE Wolves. He had to be kidding.

"Ha ha," I said. "Good one, as if they would really send three hundred werewolves out after Monty and me."

"Closer to five hundred, Strong," Ramirez said. "They're pissed and they're sending a message."

Once the DCE are sent out, it's usually way past the time for conversation. To send out five hundred werewolves against Monty and me meant the Dark Council was serious. The message was clear: *You stand against us, we will eliminate you with overwhelming numbers and force.*

Part of me was impressed that we had pissed off the Dark Council to this extent. The effort it took to mobilize a battalion and deploy them in the city was considerable. The other—saner—part of me ran off into a corner, screaming that this was the end.

"We've crossed paths before," I said. "They aren't fans."

"Fans? They *hate* your agency," Ramirez said. "This is the chance they've been waiting for. Especially the wolves, after what happened with Davros."

Some time ago, a psycho mage named Davros had controlled a bunch of werewolves and had tried to erase us. Most of the werewolf community blamed Davros, but a few of them felt it was our fault. It didn't make sense, but who said irrational hatred had to make sense?

Werewolves held grudges. It wasn't something I could do anything about, except stay out of their way. Out of the three factions, weres were the most private. They kept to themselves and rarely interacted with humans.

Each faction of the Dark Council had a branch of the DCE: mages, vampires, and wolves. Out of the three, the wolves were the most dangerous, ruthless, and relentless.

When the threat was large enough, they'd send out a mixed legion comprised of all three. I suppose we were lucky they hadn't gotten to that point yet. A were-only response meant that the other two factions were holding back…for now. It was clear they were overreacting.

A battalion of DCE Wolves against one angry Montague? I almost felt sorry for the werewolves. I needed to speak to Chi before this got out of hand and Monty melted them all.

That would really escalate things.

TWENTY-FOUR

"WHO'S LEADING THE pack, do you know?"

"The memo was light on the details," Ramirez answered. "NYTF is expected to assist on this one. Take your wizard, your monster dog, and get the hell out of my city."

"Working on it," I said. "Thank you for the heads up. I owe you one."

"One?" Ramirez barked. "You owe me one, followed by several zeros! I'm serious, Strong. DCE is insane and they smell blood. Get out now…while you still can."

"Got it, thanks." I hung up and stepped inside the Randy Rump.

Monty was sitting at a far table, sipping from a steaming cup. I looked around and noticed the place was empty except for Jimmy behind the counter. He nodded as I walked in and scanned the room.

Jimmy the Cleaver was a large man. He stood behind the counter, arms crossed, his long gray hair pulled back in a ponytail. He wore an apron over a T-shirt and jeans. His massive arms, which were easily the size of my legs, were covered with thick hair. As a werebear, I'd never seen him in animal form. Considering his size, I probably didn't want to.

The only time I'd seen the Rump this empty, Jimmy had been having a heated conversation with an unsanctioned vampire Resolution Team. It hadn't ended well for them. The Randy Rump became a neutral location soon after that, and I scored free meat for life.

Aside from Ezra's, the Randy Rump was Peaches' idea of Hellhound heaven. He chuffed and gave Jimmy a low woof of greeting. Jimmy answered with a low growl and Peaches approached his usual spot.

<Do you think Bearman can give me meat?>

<He certainly can. In fact, that's what he does. For Jimmy… Meat is Life.>

<Only because he knows what's important. Please ask him for the extra meat you promised.>

<Will do, boy. Just don't eat too much. Something feels weird and I don't want you too full to move.>

<Too much? What does that mean? How can I eat too much meat? Will you remember to ask for extra?>

It amazed me that my Hellhound could forget some of the simplest things from one second to the next, yet remember meat-based conversations for hours.

I walked up to the counter and turned to face the main seating area. After the renovations, the Randy Rump had gone from butcher shop to a butcher shop, restaurant, and meeting hall.

"Load him up," I said, patting Peaches on his head. "Slow night?"

"Death Wish?" Jimmy asked, grabbing a mug. "Extra death?"

I nodded. Death Wish-extra death meant that he used freshly brewed coffee instead of water to brew a new pot. Not recommended for the faint of heart.

Jimmy placed a large titanium bowl, overflowing with pastrami, on the floor. The bowl was etched with a large letter P and matched the one Ezra kept for Peaches in his shop.

I couldn't shake the sense of unease at seeing the Rump empty. Something felt off. Monty sat quietly sipping his tea. Judging from his expression, he was thoroughly enjoying his orlandgasmic experience.

During the day, there were no less than ten mage guards standing or sitting in strategic locations throughout the seating area.

By nightfall, the mage guards were replaced with vampires or shifters of some sort. The Dark Council took the safety and neutrality of its designated locations seriously.

Leaving a neutral location unprotected like this was unheard of…unless the Rump had lost its neutral status.

Neutral locations never closed their doors. They provided sanctuary for anyone inside their space. Combat, spell casting, or any type of violence was forbidden. Violating the established rules of neutral locations could end in permanent retirement…from life.

I leaned against the counter as the smell of coffee filled my lungs. Death Wish-infused javambrosia was the equivalent of being punched in the face by a squadron of angels who sang a heavenly choir, as the coffee pummeled your senses into blissful submission.

Yes, I loved my coffee.

"Death Wish, heavy on the death," Jimmy said, setting the mug on the counter behind me. I pulled out my flask and poured a teaspoonful in the mug. Jimmy raised an eyebrow and shook his head, as I sighed at the combined aroma. "You and that coffee should get a room."

I grabbed the mug, said a reverent thanks to Caffeina, my patron goddess of coffee, and sipped divine javambrosia.

"Are we having a holiday I'm unaware of?" I asked between sips. "You gave everyone the night off?"

"We're closed early for renovations," Jimmy said, giving me a look.

"Renovations? The place looks great. What do you need to renovate?"

"You have a guest waiting for you in the office," Jimmy replied. "He suggested I empty the Rump tonight since you and Tristan were on your way."

"On our way?" I asked, confused. "No one knew we were coming here."

"He did," Jimmy said, taking off his apron. "I was just waiting for you to get here. Just so you know, I really like this place. I've never banned a customer, or a friend, from my business, but every time you two show up—well, I'd appreciate it if you visited less."

"Understood," I said as Jimmy walked to the door. He closed it behind him and placed a hand on the frame. Runes, inscribed throughout the Randy Rump, flashed with an orange glow. I raised my mug, he nodded in return, and walked away into the night.

Peaches padded over to where I stood. His enormous head nudged my leg, nearly launching me across the Rump.

<Are you full? Or is that not even possible with that black hole you call a stomach?>

<I need to eat to stay strong.>

I rubbed the side of my leg.

< I don't think you have to worry about getting stronger. How was the meat?>

<That was good. I like the Bearman.>

<You like the meat Bearman gives you, that's what you like.>

<That too. I will have to give him a lick thank you.>

<How about I just thank him for you? That way you can save your licks for emergencies.>

Monty had finished his tea and stood in front of the office door, waiting for me.

"What did Ramirez want?"

"Dark Council is sending DCE after us."

Monty flexed his jaw. "How many factions?"

"Wolves—for now."

"This behavior is completely irrational," Monty said. "Can you call your vampire?"

"I think I'm going to have to," I said. "They're going to send out one—"

"One squad? Really, they have the audacity to send out a squad? After us?"

"One battalion."

"Bloody hell," he said quietly. "I'm almost impressed. Are you certain this isn't personal? Have you angered your vampire?"

"Sure, Monty," I snapped. "I pissed off Chi so much she felt the need to send out five hundred DCE Wolves to kick my ass."

"Stranger things have happened," Monty replied with

a tug of his sleeve. "We'll have to address that later. Did Ramirez say when they would deploy?"

"A few days."

"Very well," Monty said with a nod. "If the Dark Council wants a war, we'll bloody their nose and hope they lose heart."

"And if they don't?" I asked, not really wanting to hear his answer. "What if they don't back down?"

"Then we will decimate them and teach them respect," Monty answered, his voice steel. "They will reconsider counting a Montague as an enemy."

Like I said, an angry Montague was a scary thing.

I shook my head and focused on the task at hand. We needed to see who was expecting us.

I narrowed my eyes and saw that Jimmy had added to the runes since our last visit. Magical inscriptions covered every inch of the door's surface.

This door, even though it wasn't as strong as the back-room door, was still impressive. It stood eight feet tall and half as wide, making it easy for the werebear to enter his office without stooping.

"Ready?" Monty asked as he pressed the runes in sequence. He pulled on the handle. "I'd hate to keep our guest waiting."

It swung open easily and I looked inside. A large desk sat against the far wall, opposite the door. To the right of the desk and along the wall sat a large brown sofa. On the other side of the desk, against the left wall, I saw two tall, black filing cabinets.

Jimmy kept his desk neat, with several piles of papers in organized stacks along the surface. An industrial-sized computer monitor took up almost half the desk.

On the back wall, I saw the new door. This door was a smaller version of the main door in the butcher shop, securing the entrance to the back room.

The door and frame were made of Australian Buloke ironwood. I narrowed my eyes and saw that it, too, was magically inscribed with new runes on every inch of its surface.

Most of the runes on the door were indecipherable. The few I did understand scared the hell out of me. Jimmy had increased the configurations. If anyone tried to use this door without knowing the sequence, they were in for a world of pain, right before the failsafe obliterated them.

"Those runes," I said with dawning recognition, "those are protractor runes."

"Proto-runes," a voice said as the door opened to the back room. "Gentlemen, come in. We have much to plan and precious little time to do it in."

It was Hades.

TWENTY-FIVE

"THAT PORTAL SWALLOWED you whole," I said as the door closed behind us. "The Lucent snatched you."

The back room of the Rump was considerably smaller than the front area. It consisted of one large room with three tables.

Two of them, placed along the north and south walls, were long and rectangular. The third table, placed in the center, was round. Each of them had seating for seven. Each table was heavy, dark oak, and inscribed with runes along its surface. Hades moved over to the center table.

Monty narrowed his eyes and stared at him.

"Yes." Hades looked down at Peaches and gave him a small nod. "They did indeed. They just couldn't keep me."

"You *let* them take you," Monty said. "It was too late to activate the gate in your office. Why is your energy signature bifurcated?"

"It was the only way I could use the gate back,"

Hades replied. "Am I to assume my office has been destroyed?"

I looked at Monty. "The Lucent threw a building-melter and erased your office," I said. "We tried to stop it. My magic missile wasn't very effective."

Hades nodded. "As expected," he said. "They were trying to prevent my return here."

"They knew about the gate, which means you have a traitor in your midst," Monty said. "It wasn't Corbel, or this gate would have been compromised as well."

"Corbel would never betray me," Hades answered. "My traitor is a little closer to home and will be dealt with—in time."

"You know who it is?" I asked. "Why not deal with them now?"

"I do and they will regret their betrayal, but I must leave them in place for now."

"*You* were the signature I sensed in the lobby," Monty said with a sudden realization. "You disguised a teleportation circle and came here to the Rump?"

"Why not just port here?" I asked. "It would have been faster."

"If a Lucent was still near the building, they would have followed him," Monty answered. "By splitting his signature, going to the lobby, and then teleporting here, he threw the Lucent off his trail."

"It also allowed me to locate Persephone before returning."

"The portal the Lucent cast led to Tartarus," Monty said. "But you had the backup made. That's how you knew we'd come here."

"Well done, Tristan," Hades said. "The portal led to

Tartarus— and to Persephone, my wife. I instructed Corbel to inform you of this gate if anything happened to me. After that, it was only a matter of time."

"Once you broke free, you came here, but you couldn't leave," Monty said, looking around the back room. "The runic signature of this place effectively hides you. If you left, the Lucents would have tracked you down and trapped you again, especially in your diminished state."

"Or worse, moved Persephone," Hades said. "Right now, they think I'm in a cell. I need them to keep thinking that."

"You left your energy signature in place?" I asked, confused. "How is that even possible?"

"I'd try explaining it to you, but it would melt your brain."

I stared at Hades. "Do you know a mage named Ziller?"

"Why didn't you bring Persephone?" Monty asked.

"You said you know where she is," I said. "Why not break her out?"

"I had no choice," Hades said, his expression dark, reminding me that I was speaking to a god. A powerful one who could probably kill me a few times before he got bored. "Tartarus was still too close. I couldn't risk releasing her without my weapon."

"Why do you need a weapon?" I asked. "You're a god. You can just…I don't know…cast some power. Hit them with lightning or something."

"I think you're confusing me with my brother," Hades answered. "I need my bident, *Kathon,* to release Persephone and seal the gate to Tartarus."

"The proto runes," Monty said. "They affect you."

Hades nodded. "My bident is made of a special material. When my brother discarded Cronus' scythe, parts of it were scattered and fashioned into weapons."

"The Kamikira," Monty said. "Are they—?"

"Those are diminished aspects of the scythe," Hades said. "*Kathon* is not an alloy. It is made only of proto-steel."

"Your bident is made from the same material as the scythe?" Monty asked, surprised. "*That* is what Tartarus wants."

Hades nodded. "With it, he can escape his domain and destroy all who dare oppose him," Hades answered. "With my bident, I can keep him in Tartarus, where he belongs."

"Why can't we just destroy the gate here and trap him in Tartarus?" I asked, thinking the less exposure to a homicidal primordial being the better. "That way we keep our plane safe and he stays down there. Away from us."

"Two things, Strong," Hades said. "You're forgetting Persephone. And in order to seal the gate to Tartarus, it must be done from the inside."

"From…the inside? This is a suicide run?"

"Not for him," Monty said, pointing at Hades. "He has a way."

"My power is greatly diminished in Tartarus. The realm is designed to imprison beings like me. But you have managed to do something I didn't think possible."

"What?" I asked, wary. "What did Monty do now?"

Monty glared at me.

"You have managed to get his attention," Hades said.

"To the extent that he is coming to destroy you personally."

"As flattering as that sounds, this is where we call it a day," I said. "One primordial psycho is enough to last me millennia. Monty?"

"Where is this Kathon?" Monty asked. "Where is your weapon? Do you know its locat—?"

"No," I interrupted. "Why are we asking where his weapon is? We don't *want* to know where the weapon is. This is god business. Last I checked, we weren't gods."

"Of course," Hades answered, ignoring me. "In my home, in the safest place I could think of."

"Some kind of god vault with impenetrable walls? Hidden in the deepest recesses of the Underworld?"

"No, I said the *safest* place," Hades replied with a smile. "A vault, even one in the Underworld, could not contain Kathon for long."

"What would be safer than a super vault? Maybe a trans-dimensional space, time-shifting plane?"

"You clearly have been reading too much fiction," Hades answered with a shake of his head. "Kathon is hanging around his father's neck."

Hades pointed at Peaches.

"You're saying Cerberus is wearing your weapon?" I asked, looking at Peaches. "Your Hellhound, *the* Hellhound, is holding your weapon?"

"I did say the safest place," Hades replied, sitting in one of the chairs. "I can't retrieve Kathon in my current state."

"That's a real shame," I said, heading for the door. "I don't think Monty knows a teleportation circle to Hades. You don't, right, Monty?"

"No, I don't," Monty answered. "No circles to Hades exist that I'm aware of."

"There, you see? Really wish we could've helped, but this is way above our paygrade," I said. "Why not ask your brothers? They're ultra-heavy hitters."

"My brothers would never take action against Tartarus," Hades said. "I'm not exactly close to them these days. *You* will have to retrieve Kathon for me."

"You're using us as bait," Monty said. "That is what this is."

"I don't need you to *defeat* Tartarus," Hades replied. "I just need you to *distract* him long enough for me to get Persephone and seal his domain."

"Well, doesn't *that* sound familiar," I said, glancing at Monty. "It still won't work. It's not like we can take a cab to Hades."

"You don't need to." Hades looked at Peaches. "You have the method of travel right there."

"Peaches?"

"Yes," Hades said. "Even though he is bound to you, with a little help, I can show him how to go home."

"You said it was too dangerous," I answered, "that Cerberus would try to destroy him."

"Then I suggest you find a way to get Kathon while my Hellhound is distracted," Hades said. "The moment you enter the Underworld, Tartarus will come for you."

"What? You want us to bring monster sausage to feed Cerberus?" I asked. "Somehow I don't think that would work."

"I have an idea," Monty said. "But we're going to need room."

TWENTY-SIX

"HOW LARGE IS Cerberus?" Monty asked. "Would he fit in this room?"

Hades shook his head. "Impossible, Cerberus dwarfs this structure. He guards the gates of Hades, mage. He is a large creature."

"He shares a bond with you, correct?"

Hades nodded. "Similar to Strong and his Hellhound. Only one forged over millennia."

"If we open a portal and you exit this room, would he come to you?"

"Without question," Hades answered. "Followed by the Lucent and Tartarus."

"In order to come at you, Tartarus will have to do what Chaos did and engage in corporeal personification, yes?"

"It's a good plan, mage, but even in that state, he will be too powerful for you, Strong, and two Hellhounds—even if one of those is Cerberus," Hades said, shaking his head. "I will not be able to assist you. My power and abilities would be no match for Tartarus."

"I intend on having more than just us waiting for Tartarus," Monty said, looking at me. "We'll have a small army waiting for Tartarus. How long do you need to rescue Persephone and seal Tartarus?"

"Once I have Kathon in my possession, ten minutes at most to locate my Persephone, get her to safety, and seal the gate."

"Do you have the energy signature for your weapon?" Monty asked.

"Yes, of course."

"Is it detailed enough to make a simulacra?" Monty asked. "Can you imbue it with enough of the original energy signature to be convincing?"

"As long as it's not wielded," Hades said, "it can convince anyone it is authentic—until it is touched."

"We can buy you ten minutes. Give us a moment."

Monty pulled me over to the side.

"Clearly you've lost your mind," I hissed. "Have you forgotten how close to dying we were when we faced Chaos?"

"What do you think will happen if Tartarus gets his hands on Hades' weapon?"

"Primordial being wipes out self-important gods and takes their domains for himself. Sounds like a happy ending."

"Simon, I know you aren't fond of gods, but—"

"Aren't fond?" I scoffed. "Gods don't care about *us*. We're pawns. Pieces to be used in their cosmic games and then discarded. He admitted it just now—we're bait."

"Tartarus won't stop with the gods," Monty said quietly. "Once he destroys them, he'll come for the supernaturals, and then the humans. Beings like Tartarus are never satisfied. We have to stop him."

Monty was right, but that didn't mean I had to like it.

"Shit. Fine," I said with a grunt. "What's your plan?"

"I'm going to need you to make a call."

Monty's plan was insane, but solid. We were going to leave the Randy Rump and relocate to the 14th Street Park. The park was located between 14th and 15th Streets and took up a square block from 10th to 11th Avenues.

In the center of the park was a large oval field of grass where Monty planned to summon Cerberus, get the Kathon, give it to Hades, and face off against Tartarus.

I would stay back and work with Hades to create a portal for Cerberus to join his bondmate. I wasn't looking forward to meeting Papa Peaches.

Before we created the portal and Monty runed the park, I just had one thing to do: I had to convince Chi that Monty wanted to erase the city.

"When she finds out this was a ruse, she's going to want to kill me," I said, watching Hades trace the runes on Peaches' flank. Every time he touched one it would glow for a few seconds and then fade. "Repeatedly."

"Good thing death isn't a permanent issue for you," Monty said with an almost smile. "Try to be convincing. She needs to believe I've gone dark and mad from blood magic use. You know, insane mage bent on destroying everything."

"Shouldn't be too hard of a sell," I said. "What if this doesn't work?"

"We don't dwell on that," Monty answered. "It is a

mistake to look too far ahead. Only one link in the chain of destiny can be handled at a time."

I nodded. "Plans are worthless, but planning is everything," I answered. "British bulldog never fails."

"Indeed," Monty said with a nod. "Remember the timing. I'll rune the park and set the containment perimeter. When you feel the shift, that's when you come out with Hades."

"And I'll feel this shift? Are you sure? Even in here?"

"Every supernatural below 14th Street will feel this shift."

"Won't it attract the Lucent?"

"I believe that's the point," Monty said. "We want them on their way by the time Hades appears. Besides, I need to give your vampire something credible, to corroborate your story."

"Do I want to know what it is you're going to be casting in the park?"

"Not really, no. Suffice it to say, it *will* feel like I'm trying to take the city with me."

"Because you're going to create a *fake* spell that feels like you're trying to erase the city, right?" I said. "No crazy-ass blood magic spells that siphon your lifeforce and leave you a dried-out raisin?"

"Do you want the truth, or elaborate lies that will make you feel better?"

I remembered my conversation with Roxanne:

"You want me to shoot Monty with a magic missile?"

"If you see him attempting to use blood magic again, yes,"

There was no way I was going to shoot Monty, blood magic or not. If Roxanne found out, I'd have an angry sorceress to add to the list of people wanting to shred and maim me. Wonderful.

"Roxanne wanted me to stop you from using blood magic," I said. "Even enhanced my magic missile."

"I know. Your energy signature reads differently. She means well, but I'm afraid it wasn't much of an enhancement."

"You could sense that?"

"Remember when I mentioned the Tomatis effect?" Monty asked. "I *know* Roxanne's signature. The magic missile you know is not sorcery. When she tried to enhance your ability, she may as well have announced what she was doing."

"So she didn't really improve my magic missile?"

"I'm afraid your missile is still quite underpowered. Only practice will overcome that. There are no shortcuts in magic. Those who try to use them learn that right away, or they die horrible deaths."

"Practice it is, then," I said quickly. "What did she do then?"

"Her 'enhancement' will actually allow her to determine the use of blood magic in your proximity," Monty answered. "She's trying to keep an eye on me, and you too, it seems."

I shook my head. "Clever. I never would've guessed that."

"Do not underestimate her, she is a powerful sorceress," Monty replied. "This is why you will join me *after* I prepare the park."

"You sure you want to do it this way? If Chi believes me, the park will be a warzone."

"This way will keep out the NYTF and local law enforcement. Once the Dark Council mobilizes, they'll cordon the area around the park for several blocks in every direction."

"Minimal-to-no human collateral damage," I said. "And if Chi doesn't believe me?"

"She will. I won't give her a choice," Monty answered. "I'll also try to make your story convincing, which will prevent your dismemberment afterwards. If there is an afterwards."

"Well, I'm all cheered up now," I said. "If this mage thing doesn't work out, you can always take up motivational speaking. You have a way with words."

"Simon, mages don't get to be old by being optimists. We're realists and try to see things as they are without adding any meaning or emotion."

"Right, you're saying mages are Vulcans. Got it."

"Spock would've made an exceptional mage."

"Dex isn't cold and calculating," I replied. "He's the most emotional mage I know. Not that my pool of mages is large."

"I explained about my uncle."

"He's insane?"

"Exactly," Monty said. "And much older than any mage *I* know. There are things about him that I'm still learning."

"This just feels like a doomsday scenario," I said. "More than our usual doomsday scenario."

"How so?" Monty asked, examining the door to the back room for the runic sequence. "I'd imagine by now a doomsday scenario would feel familiar."

"If I call Chi, we can start a war, and our lives are in danger," I said. "If I don't, we get to face Tartarsauce alone and our lives are in danger. Sounds like the same outcome."

"Except that in one, we fight for our lives with an army, and in the other we allow Tartarus to take our lives."

I nodded. "I'll take option one. Meet you at the park."

Monty left the Rump to prep the park. Being a block away still felt like ground zero. I hoped the Randy Rump was far enough away from the park that 'Jimmy the Butcher' wouldn't come back to a crater.

"You're a god," I said, looking at Hades once Monty had gone. "Why would *you* need help from us, insignificant humans?"

Hades stared at me. I was certain that even in his 'diminished state' he could still smear me all over the floor with little effort. His energy signature, even broken into parts, was still off-the-charts scary. If I had to ascribe a numerical value to it from zero to nine thousand, I'd say it was easily over nine thousand.

"Who said you were insignificant?"

"I know you and your type."

"Do you now?" Hades said with a slight smile. "Enlighten me."

I was pissed, but I kept my anger in check. It was true that he needed us, but even a god must have limits to his patience. I wasn't trying to find those limits tonight.

"You're giving us just enough information to know what kind of shitstorm is coming, but there are still a few details left out."

"Like?" Hades continued tracing the runes on Peaches' flank.

"Like why target you?" I started. "Why not steal your weapon from Cerberus first? Why kidnap Persephone? Why make a move to steal Hades?"

"Peaches is ready," Hades said, patting him on the flank, "and I will indulge you, seeing as how you may die several times tonight."

"That's encouraging."

"I'm the god of the Underworld, Strong. I don't do encouraging."

"Noted," I said. "Indulge away."

"Tartarus targeted me because, out of the three siblings, I am the greatest threat," Hades said. "I'm also the closest."

"You're more of a threat than your brothers, really?"

"I'm the god of the Underworld. Everything dies—eventually. Even gods. One day they will all be in my domain—all of them."

I thought for a moment, then I realized what drove his family to distance themselves.

"They're *scared* of you, aren't they?"

"Comes with the territory," Hades answered with a shrug. "Mortals, unlike you, have made peace with the fact that they will perish one day. Gods? Immortals? They're frightened to death—about death."

"Why don't they just steal your weapon from Cerberus?"

Hades looked down at Peaches and rubbed his head. "Have you met Cerberus?"

"Can't say I've had the pleasure, no."

"Imagine Peaches here, not a puppy as he is now."

It still boggled my mind that Peaches was considered a puppy. At the rate he was going, I'd need a herd of cattle to keep him fed.

"Hard to do, but okay. Peaches as an adult sounds like a scary thought."

"It is," Hades said. "In his full-grown battlemode, he will be five times larger than his present battlemode is now. He will have his baleful glare, indestructible skin, and teleportation, in addition to other abilities."

"Other abilities?"

"I'd rather you discover those on your own, as I'd hate to ruin the surprise," Hades said. "That being said, in his domain, Cerberus is indestructible. Tartarus would avoid a direct confrontation with my Hellhound."

"And the weapon?"

"I've camouflaged my bident around Cerberus' neck. It looks like a type of tuning fork. It's completely masked and undetectable."

"Hiding in plain sight."

"If by plain sight you mean around the neck of the guardian to the Underworld, then yes. Hiding in plain sight."

"Why Persephone?"

Hades' face grew dark, and I felt the shift of energy radiate off him in waves. He clenched his fists and, after a few seconds, released them.

"She's my vulnerability," Hades answered after a few seconds of silence. "I'm not like my brothers. They've sired countless demigods. I've preferred not to overpopulate the planes with my seed."

"TMI," I said, shaking my head. "Way too much info, but I get it. You manage to keep it in your pants."

"By taking Persephone, he took what is most

precious to me," he said, keeping his voice low. "He knows how I feel about her and knows what I would do to get her back."

"This thing you have with Mrs. Hades…"

"Thing?" Hades asked, and I felt a wave of subtle energy slide off him and fill the room. "You will want to consider your next words carefully, Strong."

I nodded. I remembered that even though he looked human, this was a god. A god whose wife had just been kidnapped from him and held prisoner by a being who wanted to trade her for a world-ending weapon.

"There are several accounts about how your wife ended up in Hades," I started slowly. "But they all agree that you—how do I put this delicately—saw Persephone, fell in love, and absconded with said beauty."

"Not every myth is accurate, Strong," Hades answered. "You'd be surprised at the myths I've heard."

"Really? Myths like…?"

It was a deft deflection, but I figured I shouldn't push the issue. The fact was, he kidnapped Persephone and took her to Hades. They worked out a deal later, where she would only spend six months in Hades. Supposedly, she grew to love him too, but the relationship had begun with a kidnapping.

Talk about stealing her breath away…

"There is the one about the tactless immortal detective who, upon angering a god of the Underworld, was tortured to the brink of death, over and over. He experienced every wound and excruciating moment. This went on for centuries—until it ended."

"How did it end?" I asked, because I was nothing if

not suicidal. "The immortal detective thwarted the angry god, kicked his ass, and escaped?"

"No, I'm afraid that myth ended poorly for the immortal." Hades shook his head. "He never broke free and spent the rest of his days undergoing the Prometheus treatment. One day, the angry god took pity on him and disintegrated the immortal, scattering his remains among the dead."

"The Prometheus treatment?"

"With a twist," Hades said with a grim smile. "The immortal was chained to the gates of Hades, where Cerberus devoured his perpetually regenerating intestines every day. There, the immortal served as a warning to others, and an eternal meal to the Hellhound. Where he spent the rest of his days of life as meat."

The tone of his voice chilled my blood and I figured this was one myth not worth revisiting.

"You know what, why don't we leave the whole 'kidnapping Persephone' topic for another day?"

"Wise choice," Hades said with a smile. "It should be enough to know that Tartarus will feel my fury once he is secured in his domain. He thinks that by holding her, I will trade my weapon for her freedom."

"Wouldn't that be easier?" I asked. "You give him the tuning fork, he gives you Mrs. Hades. End of story."

"Yes, right up to the point when he storms the gates of Hades and destroys everything with my own weapon," Hades said. "After that, he'll pay my brothers a visit, wipe them out, and then where do you think he'll visit next?"

"Can't you just destroy this weapon?"

"This isn't the one ring, Strong. Proto-steel is more energy than steel. Energy can't be destroyed, only transformed."

"That means no forge toss?"

"None," Hades answered. "Reuel took considerable artistic license in his solution to that particular problem. If it was as simple as tossing Kathon into lava or the heart of a star, I would have done so millennia ago."

"Why do you gods create these weapons of destruction?"

Hades smiled. "Humans aren't so different," Hades said. "Innovation leads to weaponization, which leads to destruction."

"The only difference, "I said, "is that we don't go around creating indestructible weapons."

"Really?" Hades asked. "*Now I become Death, the destroyer of worlds*, is not a reference to me, you know."

"Touché," I said, realizing he was right. "Except *we* aren't gods, and we don't possess supernatural abilities[But they do. ??]."

"Tell me," Hades said, "when you heard the Dark Council was coming for Tristan, who were you concerned for, honestly?"

"You know what? You suck."

"Says the immortal, Hellhound-bound, time-stopping detective." Hades looked down at my thigh sheath. "Did I miss anything?"

"You forgot my energy-siphoning blade."

"No, I didn't," Hades answered. "You are closer to us than you think. The fact is, weapons like the Kathon exist first as an innovation, and later on as checks and balances."

"So you're saying we need a god-killing blade?"

"How do you plan on stopping a primordial entity bent on destroying everything?" Hades asked. "You can't reason with him. There's no appealing to his sense of justice or fair play. The only way to stop him is to thwart his goals or total annihilation. Preferably his."

"Point made and taken," I said. "I'd like to avoid any annihilation—total or otherwise."

"Then we'd better get my weapon and stop Tartarus before he removes any obstacles."

"And by *obstacle,* you mean Monty and me?"

A few seconds later, small tremors shook the Rump, followed by a long foghorn of sound, rising in volume until the small tremors became violent shaking. Peaches whined next to me, shaking his head.

"What the hell is that?"

"That would be Tristan undoing the fabric of space and time around Manhattan," Hades answered calmly. "I think you'd better make that call."

TWENTY-SEVEN

"IT'S MONTY," I said, nearly yelling into my phone as the foghorn sound blared around me. "He's lost his mind."

"What happened?" Chi asked. Behind her, I could hear the noise of activity and orders being barked in the background. "Is he responsible for the energy signature fluctuation downtown? Where are you?"

"He said no one is going to erase or incarcerate him," I answered. "I tried to convince him to turn himself in. He said he'd rather take most of the city with him before allowing anyone to erase him. I'm in the Randy Rump."

"He's lost his mind."

"I think it's the blood magic," I said, feigning concern. "I warned him it was dangerous, but I'm not a mage. He's been violent as of late, destroying things just for the sake of it."

"He must be stopped," she answered, her voice dark. "Do not approach him, Simon. It's not safe. That person is not the mage you know. His mind has been subverted by dark magic."

"I don't recognize him anymore," I answered, allowing just the right amount of fear to fill my voice. "He said something about unleashing some primordial being on the city."

Hades raised an eyebrow and gave me an approving nod. Part of me felt bad about lying. The other part remembered how the Dark Council intended to erase and euthanize those closest to me—my family. That part grabbed the first part in a chokehold and put it down mercilessly.

No one threatened my family…no one.

"Stay in the Rump, Simon," Chi barked. "Let the Council deal with this."

"I feel like I should be there, maybe talk him down."

"Absolutely not. Under no circumstance are you to approach the mage. Is that understood?"

"I understand," I said. "I just thought—"

"No!" Chi barked. "Stay put. I have battalions in place to deploy. We will be there inside ten minutes. The Dark Council will deal with this."

She hung up and I looked from my phone to Hades.

"There goes Monty's army."

"They won't be enough, not against Tartarus and his Lucent."

"Like you said, they don't need to defeat him," I answered, my voice hard, "just distract him."

"Indeed," Hades answered. "I'd say it's a good thing you can't die, because when she finds out what you've done—"

"She's going to kill me."

"Repeatedly," he added. "Painfully as well. She wasn't

called the Reaping Wind for nothing. I'm certain she knows how to inflict immense amounts of pain in the most—"

"Got it," I said, raising a hand. "She's going to kill me. It's going to hurt. Rinse and repeat."

"Look at it this way," Hades replied as he headed for the door, "we never did get to test the limits of your immortality. I think Ms. Nakatomi's response will be an excellent opportunity."

"I'd rather face a swarm of angry dragons," I said, rubbing Peaches' head as he padded over. "At least with them, I have an idea of what to expect."

"No, you don't," Hades said, touching the runes in sequence. "But you may be right. The dragons would be preferable to an angry, ancient vampire who loves you and feels betrayed."

"The Dark Council threatened to erase Monty and kill Peaches," I said. "I'm doing what I can to make sure that doesn't happen. If that means standing against Michiko, then so be it."

Hades gave me an appraising look.

"Once I leave this room, it will be like sending the Lucent a beacon," Hades said. "They will be actively searching for me by now."

"I thought you said they think you're in a cell?"

Hades nodded. "The Lucent in Tartarus have no reason to suspect I'm missing. The Lucent here will be alerted to my unique signature and will investigate."

"Once they see you—?"

"They will try and alert their counterparts in Tartarus," Hades said. "We can't let that happen. I'll use Kathon to stop them."

"What about Tartarus himself? Won't he know you're all over the place?"

"By the time I left, he had manifested corporeally and was planning on paying you and the mage a visit," Hades answered. "Traveling in that state limits his power and ability."

"He has to get information like the rest of us," I said. "So he's coming for us. Why?"

"Aside from destroying a Lucent, which is quite an insult considering you are both human, Tristan's latest shift has increased his power to such a degree that he can't hide any longer."

"And me?" I asked, thinking there was no real reason for a primordial being to target me. "I'm not much of a threat."

"You're the chosen of Kali, a cursed human, bound to a Hellhound," Hades said, counting on fingers. "You speak to a personification of causality, and occasionally stop time, while wielding the closest thing to a god-killer a human can hold."

"Well, shit."

"Yes. Between Tristan almost becoming an Arch Mage, give or take a few centuries, and an immortal human who manages to anger almost every being he comes across, I'd say hiding will be next to impossible."

"Once we step out, how long before Tartarus shows up?"

"Giving what Tristan has started, he should be on his way, along with the Dark Council," Hades answered. "The Lucent will arrive before Tartarus, and we will summon Cerberus once we get to the park."

"This plan has too many moving parts," I said.

"Something is bound to get screwed."

"No plan survives first contact with the enemy," Hades said. "Moltke knew what he was talking about. When it all goes pear-shaped, adapt. This is something you and Tristan excel at."

"I have one more question before we leap into this nightmare," I said. "Why didn't you just go straight to Cerberus and retrieve your weapon? Could've saved us time."

Hades paused before activating the sequence.

"In this state, my bond with Cerberus is halved."

"Halved? What do you mean halved?"

"He'll come to my location, but my control over him is reduced. It will be similar to what you experienced in London when your bond with Peaches was shattered."

"Are you saying we're bringing your Hellhound here and that you won't be able to control him?"

"Control? No. Suggest, possibly." Hades began the sequence. "At least until I get Kathon. Once I have my weapon, he will follow me."

"Follow or hunt?"

"Closer to hunt," Hades said with a smile, finishing the sequence. "Semantics. Either way, he'll be upset, follow, and try to get the weapon back—violently."

"Oh, bloody hell," I said. "We are so dead."

TWENTY-EIGHT

HADES OPENED THE door and the energy from Monty's spell slammed into us. The air felt charged, like stepping into an electric current.

We ran out of the Rump. I managed two steps before the street blinked out and reappeared. We stood at the edge of the park.

I looked at Hades, who shook his head.

<*Was that you, boy?*>

<*No, that was the angry man.*>

I looked around and saw Monty in the midst of a swirling orb of violet energy. The large orb was in the center of the grass oval. All around the perimeter of the park, large red runes pulsed with power.

"Summon Cerberus," Monty said. "The Dark Council will be here shortly."

I looked up 10th Avenue and, for a moment, my brain seized. Hordes of werewolves were running down the street. Above them, I saw vampires using the buildings and, in between them, I saw the orbs of magic being used for illumination as mages kept pace.

The most unnerving part of the spectacle was the silence. It was like watching a movie with the volume turned off. A scary, piss-in-your-pants horror movie. They were several blocks away and closing fast. I moved to the center of the oval where Monty stood.

"Monty, we have incoming!"

"We need Cerberus here, as in now," Monty said. "Hades?"

Hades stepped close to Peaches. He pressed the runes on my Hellhound's flanks in a specific sequence.

"Tell him to bring his sire here," Hades said. "Make sure you tell him to bring him here. Not to 'go to him' or else this will be a short-lived exercise in death."

<Hey, boy.>

<I don't feel so good. The man who smells like home, he did something.>

I noticed Peaches had started growing. "He's growing?"

"Summon Cerberus, Strong," Hades said, looking across the park up 11th Avenue at another matching horde of Dark Council. "Before they get here. I sense the Lucent near. We are running out of time. Tartarus can't be far behind."

<Boy, I need you to bring your father here.>

<You want me to go to my father?>

<No! I mean, no. Can you bring him here? This is very important. You need to bring him here, to us.>

<Will you let me speak to my dragon friend?>

<Are you negotiating this now? Really?>

<Frank said the best time to get what you want is when you have levers.>

<You mean leverage. I'm going to have a few words with

Frank.>

<This sounds important. Can I spend time with my dragon friend?>

When I ran into that lizard, I was going to step on him a few times.

<Yes! Yes, you can have a dragon friend. Can you bring your father here now?>

<Promise? On your word as bondmate?>

<My word as bondmate? Where did you learn that? From Frank?>

<No, that I learned from the angry man. If you give your word, you have to do it.>

<You have my word as your bondmate.>

Peaches had grown again but had not reached XL size.

<Thank you, bondmate. I will summon my sire. I suggest you step back.>

Peaches bowed his head and growled. The runes along his flanks exploded with red light as the air around him became charged with energy. He shook his body, spread his legs, and barked.

The sound deafened me for a few seconds, as all of the windows in the surrounding buildings shattered. Peaches increased in size, reaching XL status.

<MY SIRE APPROACHES. BEWARE.>

"Monty, Cerberus is on his way," I yelled. "There's only one slight problem."

"I beg your pardon?" Monty said. "What is it?"

"Hades won't be able to control him, not until he gets the weapon."

"Not control?" Monty said, whirling on Hades. "Are you insane? Bringing him here was predicated on your being able to control him."

"That detail may have slipped my mind," Hades said. "Once I have Kathon, Cerberus will lock on to me and will attempt to retrieve the weapon."

"And when you return to Tartarus to get Persephone?" Monty asked. "Will he follow you there?"

<THIS WOULD BE A GOOD TIME TO EXIT THE AREA.>

"Cerberus incoming," I said, pressing the main bead on my mala bracelet.

A large, red, swirling portal formed behind Peaches. A leg stepped through, and it took me a moment to process the enormity of what I was seeing. The leg I was looking at was taller than Peaches XL.

A low rumble filled the park, followed by the most ferocious growl I'd ever heard. Peaches turned to face the portal. He bared his teeth and growled in response.

A larger, scarier version of Peaches stepped through the portal. Overall, he was three times larger than Peaches at his largest. It was an impressive and frightening sight all at once. For a brief moment, I wondered how much sausage it would take to feed a Cerberus-sized Peaches.

Around Cerberus's neck rested a lethal, mean-looking spiked metallic collar. Hanging from the collar, I saw the upside down tuning fork that had to be Hades' weapon. All we had to do was get past all those spikes and teeth.

Cerberus raised his head and barked. I held up my shield as the sonic wave slammed into us. Peaches didn't budge against the onslaught of sound.

Hades walked up to Cerberus.

"Desist from this behavior, Cerberus," Hades said, his voice reverberating through the street. "You *will* behave."

Cerberus looked down at his bondmate and glared. Two beams of red energy slammed into Hades, launching him out of the park and onto 11th Avenue. Hades landed with a crash and formed a small crater, before standing up and dusting himself off.

As gods went, Hades was resilient, even in his diminished state. He started walking back, when a swarm of Dark Council werewolves pounced on him.

"So much for suggestion," I said. "Monty, I'm going for the tuning fork."

"Excuse me." Monty cast several orbs at the approaching Dark Council. "Duck!"

I dropped down, as several blades sliced the air above me and bounced off Monty's violet orb.

"I'm going for the weapon," I said. "Are you going to be okay in there?"

Monty nodded. "At least until Tartarus appears," Monty said. "Once he arrives, this orb will be ineffective as a deterrent."

<Boy, we need to get the tuning fork from your father's neck.>

<ARE YOU REFERRING TO KATHON, THE WEAPON ATTACHED TO HIS COLLAR?>

<Yes, the tuning fork. I'm going to need your help.>

<I STRONGLY ADVISE AGAINST THIS COURSE OF ACTION. MY SIRE IS EXPONENTIALLY STRONGER THAN I AM, WITH A GREATER ARSENAL OF WEAPONRY.>

<No choice, boy. Hades needs his tuning fork, and we need to get it to him before Tartarsauce shows up.>

<WHY ARE WE CONCERNED ABOUT CONDIMENTS? HOW DO THEY POSE A THREAT?>

<Tartarus, I mean Tartarus. We need to get the weapon before he gets here. Let's go!>

<THE ODDS OF SUCCESS ARE THREE THOUSAND SEVEN HUNDRED AND TWENTY TO ONE THAT WE WILL RETRIEVE THIS WEAPON WITHOUT SUFFERING DAMAGE.>

<Never tell me the odds.>

I ran at Cerberus, which made me reflect on the fact that, ever since I had teamed up with Monty, I was spending most of my time running *toward* creatures most people ran *away* from. I really needed a vacation.

I felt the tremor of Peaches next to me, so I grabbed his scruff and we leaped. We slipped in-between as Peaches ported. When we came back, we reappeared in front of Cerberus. Peaches managed to snap at him before Cerberus slammed us with his massive head.

We landed on the other side of the park, but Peaches wasn't moving. His breathing was ragged and I felt several broken ribs along his flank.

<C'mon, boy. You can snap out of this.>

<YOU ARE UNHARMED, GOOD. MY INJURIES WILL PREVENT ME FROM FURTHER ENGAGEMENT, BONDMATE.>

My heart seized in my chest as his breathing became more labored.

<You'll be okay. Just stay here while I go pound your father.>

<THERE IS NO NEED TO APPROACH MY SIRE. WE HAVE OUR OBJECTIVE.>

Peaches opened his mouth and spit out the tuning

fork.

TWENTY-NINE

I GRABBED THE weapon and ran to Monty.

"Drop a shield around Peaches and get this to Hades," I said. "If something happens to my Hellhound, I swear I'll go down to Tartarus myself and erase everyone."

Monty nodded and gestured. A violet dome of energy materialized over Peaches, protecting him from harm. I turned to look for Hades, when the rounds punched through me and spun me off the grass oval.

"Where is Hades?" a voice demanded. "I know he is here."

"Nilam, do not waste your time. A creature this pitiful could never slay Alnit," another voice reasoned. "It could not have been him. Perhaps the mage knows. Kill this one and question the mage."

The Lucent stepped into my field of vision with one of his guns drawn.

"Goodbye, mortal," he said, raising the gun to deliver a killing shot. "Consider yourself honored to have been slain by a servant of Tartarus, Lord of the Abyss."

I fired Grim Whisper into his groin because I was pissed. I didn't think it would get the same reaction, and it didn't, but it distracted him long enough for me to roll to the side, stagger to my feet and bury Ebonsoul in his chest.

"What are you—?" Nilam asked, using his last breath on a question that would remain forever unanswered. He looked down as I removed Ebonsoul from his chest and slashed across his neck, sending him back to wherever he came from.

The next blow came so hard and fast, I barely had time to register the pain before my face smashed into the wall of the building across the street from the park.

"Simon!" I heard Monty yell. "Hades!"

I tried to raise my arm to let him know I was okay. My arm didn't want to move no matter how many times I told it to. The heat flushed my body, and excruciating pain embraced me as I screamed in agony.

Clearly, I wasn't okay.

"You dare to touch a servant of Tartarus?" It was the third Lucent, and he didn't look happy. I guess killing his Lucent teammate surprised him. "You are unworthy of death at my hands, but I will destroy you before I return to deal with the upstart's companion."

He removed a forearm blade and stepped close.

"Today, mortal filth, I will end your existence," he said, raising the blade. "My blade will purify your blood and bring you honor. Today, you die like a warrior."

I couldn't move as he raised his arm. My body was shattered and broken. I coughed and spit up blood as I tried to speak.

"Today, it will be your honor to die like the clueless

idiot you are," I rasped. "You shouldn't have said that last part."

"You dare?" he asked, his face livid. "I will gut you like the animal you are."

"All that power, but seriously fragile egos."

"Die, scum." He brought the blade down, but it never made it to my chest. Two blades protruded from his chest as he looked down in shock. "How?"

"You tell Tartarsauce he's next," I said, groaning in agony. "As soon as I recover."

The last Lucent laughed. "Tell him yourself," he said. "He will be here shortly."

Those were his last words. Hades removed his bident, took both forearm blades, and stepped close to me.

"You realize that these blades would have killed you?" Hades asked. "As in *permanently*."

I sat up with a grimace. The realization that I'd been seconds away from a real death was sobering.

"I didn't give it thought at the time, no," I said, shaking my head. "Thanks for the assist."

"Your mouth is going to get you killed one day, Strong," Hades said, holding up his weapon. "Thank you for this."

"Where's your dog?" I said as I scanned the park.

The Dark Council was everywhere, surrounding Monty and Peaches. Monty's violet orb kept them at bay, but I saw at least twenty mages casting spells at him. Another ten were tracing runes in the air behind those twenty.

Peaches was surrounded by werewolves. They weren't touching him, but I could tell they weren't going to let him move either. Cerberus was stomping on the Dark Council. I could tell he was trying to get to Hades, but there were too many Dark Council in the way.

"Can't he just teleport over here and squash you?"

"I'm camouflaged, thanks to Kathon," Hades answered, crouching down. He reached in my inside pocket and pulled out my flask of Valhalla Javambrosia. "You need to drink all of this."

"Are you sure? Hel said never to—"

"Tartarus is close by," he said, tapping my chest with his index finger. "Drink it all. Remember, shieldbearer, I need ten minutes."

"Ten minutes tangling with a primordial being who wants to crush us like grapes—piece of cake," I said. "Any tips on dealing with him?"

"Don't die."

"Sage advice," I said with a grimace, as my body fixed more of the broken parts. "I'll keep that in mind, thanks."

"We're almost there, Strong," Hades said. "I've collected the Lucent blades. Tartarus refuses to use conventional weapons. He considers them beneath him."

"I would too, if I was that powerful," I agreed. "Any chance I could borrow yours? A god-killer would come in handy right about now."

"You have everything you need to face him—for ten minutes, at least."

"What about Peaches? Your brute of a Hellhound slammed him pretty hard."

"He'll be fine, Hellhounds are nearly impossible to kill," Hades said, looking over to where Peaches lay.

"Give him some of your flask to drink, you'll find it helps."

"I never did ask Hel what this is," I said, holding up the flask. "Do you know?"

"Of course," he said, walking away. "It's Valhalla Javambrosia."

"Smartass," I said, drinking the contents.

A pitched whistle pierced the air around the park, and Cerberus looked up, shaking off the members of the Dark Council. Hades stood in the center of 11th Avenue. He held up Kathon. It shone like a mini-sun, making it impossible to stare in his direction.

Cerberus bounded at Hades.

"He's here, Simon," Hades said. "Prepare."

"Ten minutes," I whispered to myself. I set the timer in my head and started the countdown. "Don't you dare take a second longer."

The Kathon grew even brighter, flared twice, and faded away. Hades and Cerberus were gone. An oppressive energy signature filled the area. I looked around but only saw Dark Council.

The oppressive energy signature was coming from Monty. Next to Monty, buried halfway into the ground, was Hades' bident. I had to look twice to make sure I wasn't imagining it. Every few seconds, Monty would touch it and violet energy would flare from the handle.

"Stop him!" I heard Chi yell. "He's trying to activate a void vortex. Someone get through this shield, now!"

I finished half the flask and got up. I started running to Peaches, when the lower half of the park exploded in darkness.

THIRTY

THERE WERE MOMENTS that made you question your existence. This was definitely in the top five.

I made it to Peaches, who was still lying on his side, when a cloud of malevolence engulfed the park. I scooped Peaches up and ran away. I didn't dare look back.

It felt exactly like the beginning of the syzygy. I felt helplessness and despair lingering around the edges of my consciousness. I knew if I looked back and faced him, I'd crawl into a ball and wish for death. Groups of Dark Council dropped around me. Those who dared look fell to the ground, catatonic, some in mid-scream.

The Dark Council mobilized immediately against the new threat and left Monty alone, with the mages trying to penetrate his shield.

They never stood a chance. When I felt the malevolence subside somewhat, I took a chance and glanced in his direction.

Tartarus stood at least ten feet, reminding me of a troll in stature and build. He didn't wield weapons, his fingers sliced through the Dark Council with ease.

All of his clothing was black, at least I thought it was clothing. He was enveloped in a darkness that was impossible to describe. A living cloud of energy flowed around his body, protecting him, as he obliterated any who dared to attack.

His eyes were a deep violet that swirled with energy. Several times, he just stared at attackers, causing them to fall to the ground, cowering in terror. Some gouged out their own eyes. Others used their own weapons against themselves as they screamed in terror.

The carnage was horrific, and the Dark Council was losing. I placed Peaches behind Monty's shield and patted his side. I looked at the mages trying to get through the shield and realized they were trembling with fear.

It must have taken all their resolve to stand their ground and keep trying to bring down Monty's shield.

"Get out of here," I told them. "You aren't going to bring down this shield and Tartarus is going to kill you. Do you want to die?"

A few of them shook their heads. Some wouldn't even look me in the eye.

"Go," I hissed. "Now, before it's too late."

Monty was sweating and looking worn. Every few seconds he touched the bident next to him.

"How long?" Monty asked, the strain evident in his voice. "How long do we have?"

"Seven minutes," I said, checking Grim Whisper. It was a habit. I doubted entropy rounds would do anything besides get his attention—maybe. "Can you make it?"

"If you're asking if I prefer to be elsewhere—perhaps somewhere that serves a piping hot Earl Grey, then the answer is yes."

"Tell you what," I said. "We get through this, and I'll take you to Roast, on Hades."

"On your word," Monty said with an almost smile. "The one on Stoney Street. In Southwark."

"Is there another Roast I'm not aware of?"

Unsheathing Ebonsoul, I looked down at the ground, sighed, and then raised my eyes just enough to see the death and destruction happening all around us.

"If we don't stop him," Monty said, "it will be *this* repeated everywhere. No place will be safe."

"I know. I know we can't beat him. I don't think anyone can, but we sure as hell can lock him up forever."

"Tristan Montague," Tartarus said, his voice booming across the park, "you have something that belongs to me."

"That's our cue," I said, stepping forward and pulling the pendant out from under my shirt. The enso pendant shone bright in the night. "That's new."

"It's using your lifeforce, Simon," Monty said. "How long do we have?"

"Five minutes—a lifetime," I said as Tartarus raised a fist and slammed it against the ground. The impact scattered the Dark Council in every direction. "Here he comes."

Tartarus approached. I raised Grim Whisper and fired. I emptied the magazine with no effect. The rounds never reached him, not that they would do much more than tickle him if they did.

"*You* killed my Lucent?" Tartarus asked, and I wanted to run and hide under my bed. "You speck of a human?"

I stomped down on my primal fear and stared him down. He unleashed his fear cloud, and the enso pendant increased in intensity, glowing violet and white.

"Watch Peaches while I dance with Tartarsauce," I said, holstering Grim Whisper. "We only have to do this for four and a half minutes."

I took a defensive stance and Tartarus laughed. Behind him, squads of mages launched orbs at him. All of the orbs were either absorbed by the creepy darkness around him or absorbed into his body. They may as well have been throwing cotton balls at him.

"You want to fight?" Tartarus asked, incredulous. "With me? Do you know who I am?"

"Another powerful being with an inflated ego," I said. "Same as your Lucents. They talked a good game until I ended them."

He unleashed a fist at me faster than I could track. The enso cast a shield and deflected the blow. The impact of the strike carved out a trench behind me. I smiled at his expression.

"Interesting," he said. "None have been able to withstand my fist and live."

"That's because you've only fought weaklings." I lunged, and he stepped back. I lunged again, and he moved back and smiled. "What's the matter, you scared?"

"Your blade looks dangerous," Tartarus said. "Are you sure you want to cut me?"

"Simon," Monty said, his voice urgent, "you need to

step back."

"I got this, Monty," I said, "He can't touch me. I've got my—"

Tartarus wrapped a hand around my throat. "You are a shieldbearer, are you not?"

I couldn't speak as he squeezed. I noticed the enso pendant had dimmed as my vision began to tunnel inward.

"Leave him alone," Monty said, dropping his shield and holding the bident. "You want this? Come and get it."

Tartarus dropped me and stalked to Monty.

"Monty, no!" I rasped. Tartarus had crushed most of the working parts in my throat. "Don't give it to him."

I slid forward and buried Ebonsoul into Tartarus' leg. He stopped walking and looked down at my blade. He touched the hilt and then looked at me and nodded.

"A siphon?"

I nodded. "Damn straight," I said. "Now your ass gets kicked."

"Simon, no," Monty said, his voice low. "You don't know what you've done."

Tartarus started laughing. He slid forward too fast to follow and swept Monty away from the bident. Monty sailed out of the park.

"Do you know who I am? What I am?"

"You're the being I'm about to pound into the—?"

I looked up and Tartarus laughed again. "Stupid human. You think your silly curse will keep you safe from me. I am darkness. I am the abyss. I am one of the first."

Ebonsoul exploded with darkness and my body was

filled with power—dark, primordial, evil power. I screamed until I couldn't scream anymore and still I tried to scream. The pain blinded me, and I cursed my immortality as my body exploded in heat trying to keep me alive.

"What—what are you?" I said between gasps as tears streamed down my face. My body was torn. The energy from the siphon was too much and I felt as if every cell in my body was disintegrating.

"I am your end, chosen of Kali." Tartarus removed Ebonsoul and tossed it next to me. "I will show you mercy. Take your blade and end your life."

The timer in my head told me that ten minutes were up. I really hoped Hades was a god of his word, or I was seriously going to consider ending it with Ebonsoul.

"Thank you, Lord of the Abyss," I said, grabbing Ebonsoul and getting to my knees. I placed Ebonsoul in front of my abdomen in classic seppuku position. "Your mercy is bountiful."

Tartarus reached over and grabbed the bident.

"In death you have learned what you lacked in life," Tartarus said and raised the bident over his head to deliver a killing blow. "Die with honor."

"Don't think so, Tartarsauce," I said, rolling away with a groan of pain. "Times up."

I looked around, but nothing happened. Tartarus looked around as well and nodded.

"Yes, your time is up," he said. "Time to die."

"This is what I get for trusting a god," I said. I raised my right hand and screamed, "*Ignisvitae!*"

A white beam of energy shot out from my hand and

blasted Tartarus, punching a grapefruit-sized hole through his body. He looked down in surprise and took another step toward me before the bident erupted in violet light.

"A ruse?" He screamed at me, livid. "Where is the weapon?"

I saw Monty approaching out of the corner of my eye. A burst of golden light blinded me as Hades stepped into my field of view.

"Good job, Strong," he said as I fell on my side. "I think I can take it from here."

"You're late," I answered. "Can you kick his ass now, please?"

Hades stepped forward and lunged. Tartarus dodged the attack and parried. Hades crouched and sliced upward, removing one of Tartarus' arms.

It didn't slow him down. He released his black cloud and Hades countered with a beacon of golden light.

"That weapon is rightfully mine," Tartarus said. "Return it to me."

"With pleasure," Hades said and then disappeared.

Hades blinked out and reappeared in front of a surprised Tartarus, burying the bident in Tartarus' chest. With a word from Hades, the weapon exploded with a golden light and, for a few brief seconds, we were staring at a small star.

When the light faded and I could see again, Tartarus was gone. Monty was kneeling next to me, and from the other end of the park, I could see Michiko, the leader of the Dark Council, approach.

"Would you like to deal with your angry vampire now or later?" Hades asked as he picked up Peaches.

"Later," I groaned. "Much later."

"I thought you'd respond that way."

He buried the bident into the ground in front of us and whispered another word I couldn't understand. Blue light blinded me and we were gone.

THIRTY-ONE

WHEN I REGAINED consciousness, I found myself lying in a bed the size of a small country. A fireplace burned on one side of the room and a table, covered with food, sat on the other side. Peaches snored next to the fireplace. Beside him was the largest titanium bowl I had ever seen. It had a large "C" engraved on the side.

"You're awake," said a voice from behind me. "Feel free to eat and get dressed. I'll meet you in my study."

Hades had reverted to multi-national CEO dress, with a casual suit that probably cost a fortune. He had laid out some clothes for me and I was certain he had confused me for Monty.

I didn't eat anything, even though I was starving. I seemed to remember hearing something about eating food in Hades traps you there, so I decided to play it safe.

I got dressed and woke up my Hellhound.

<Let's go, boy. We have to see Hades.>

<You smell different. Are you sick?>

I took stock of my body. I felt fine. In fact, I felt

fantastic.

<*I don't feel sick. Did you eat too much sausage?*>

<*There is no such thing as too much sausage. Not for me.*>

<*Where's Monty? Can you smell him?*>

Peaches sniffed the air for a few seconds and chuffed.

<*He is with Hades.*>

<*You know his name?*>

<*I know everyone's name, but he asked me to call him by his name.*>

<*If you know everyone's name, why do you call me bondmate?* >

<*Because that is what you are, my bondmate. That is more important than your name. You are in my pack.*>

I didn't pretend to understand Hellhound logic.

<*Lead the way to Hades, please.*>

We walked around the opulent mansion. I didn't run into any other guests, shades, or ghosts. I half-expected some undead, but I was disappointed.

We came to a large door that was slightly ajar. I overheard voices from inside. I opened the door and saw Monty, Hades, and a woman I could only assume was Persephone having a conversation.

I could see what Hades saw in Persephone. She was tall with jet-black hair and piercing eyes. Her expression was soft, but underneath I detected a core of steel.

She looked in our direction when we walked in. Her smile was radiant as she rubbed Peaches behind the ears.

"Welcome, Simon," she said. "I'm to understand you played no small part in my rescue?"

"That was mostly Hades and Monty," I said, taking a

seat in one of the large wingbacks. "I just had a conversation with Tartarus until someone"—I shot a glare at Hades—"decided to seal a gate."

"I apologize for my tardiness, Strong," Hades said. "Sealing Tartarus is not as simple as it sounds."

"Is it sealed?"

"Yes, it is. Tartarus will remain in his domain until I go pay him a visit with Kathon."

"Is that a good idea?" Monty asked. "He is still quite powerful in his own domain."

"He dared to try to use me against my love," Persephone said, and her voice went from soft to fearsome instantly. Her eyes became completely black and reverted to normal a second later. "We will both be visiting Tartarus—soon."

Now I understood why she was queen of the Underworld. In god mode, she was scarier than Hades.

"So this is Hades?" I asked, looking around. "It's a nice setup. I didn't notice any undead or dead."

"That's because you're not in Hades, Strong," Corbel said, entering the room with a plate of food. "We're on one of the islands off Tubou."

"Near Fiji?" I said, standing up and heading for the spread on the table. I almost felt as hungry as Peaches. "I thought we blinked to Hades because of the Dark Council?"

"I've spoken to the Council and explained what occurred," Hades said. "They've agreed to let you operate in the city, provided you keep the destruction to a minimum."

"Why are you looking at me?"

"Well, I smoothed things over with the Dark

Council," Hades said. "But—"

"But?"

"Your vampire resigned from her position as head of the Dark Council," Hades said. "She left the city, and her whereabouts are currently unknown."

"She's angry," I said. "And probably blames me."

"That is a very likely scenario," Hades said. "Give her time. I'm sure, once she reflects on your actions, she'll understand your motivations."

"Or she'll just try and kill me and be done with it."

"That, too, is a possibility," Hades answered with a nod. "I have urgent matters to attend to. Corbel will see to all of your needs. Please see me before you leave the island."

"What happened to the weapon?" I asked. "Did you put it someplace safe?"

"Yes." Hades nodded. "Do you feel different?"

"No, not really."

"Where is your blade?" he asked, looking at my thigh.

"What do you mean where's my blade?" I said, tapping my leg. "It's right here in my sheath."

Ebonsoul wasn't in my thigh sheath.

"You need to come to terms with your blade before it tries to do something dangerous, like kill your mage."

"Where is it?" I asked, nervous. Last thing I needed was a renegade blade out and about. "Where did you put it?"

"I didn't put it anywhere," Hades answered, heading out of the room. "You're the one who put it away."

"What about Kathon?" I asked. "Where is it now?"

"I did the same thing with Kathon that you did with

Ebonsoul," Hades said. "Trust me, it's safe."

I closed my eyes and let my senses expand. Buried deep within me, I felt Ebonsoul. It sensed my searching and reached for me. I opened my eyes.

"Seems like you found it?" Monty said, sipping his tea. "You'll have to work on controlling it, or it will control you."

"Practice?"

He nodded and sipped some more tea.

"Hours upon endless hours of practice," he said. "By the way, I think your vampire had other reasons for leaving the Dark Council."

"Besides the decimation at the hand of Tartarus and my betrayal, you mean?"

"You did not betray her," Monty said. "She was prepared to move against us, remember that. The loss of life against Tartarus is part of the job description. The Dark Council exists to keep the city safe. Even if it means at the cost of one's life."

"Then why would she resign?"

"I have solid information that a new faction of Blood Hunters are on their way."

"Blood Hunters? You mean Psycho Esti and her group?"

"The one and the same."

"What do they want? We can't return the blades without causing more bloodshed. I doubt Grey Schneider, or what's his name, is going to give up his blade. It seems I can't get rid of Ebonsoul even if I tried."

"We'll deal with that when the time comes."

"Then why are they coming back? The last time we

clashed with them, they lost their leader."

"They aren't coming *back*."

"They never left. They just went underground."

Monty nodded.

"They want the one responsible for the theft of the blades—they want the head of the *Karitori-fu*—the Reaping Wind."

"The Reaping Wind?" I asked. "That's what they used to call Chi back in Japan."

"Precisely. The Blood Hunters want the blades, but they want revenge first."

"We need to find Chi before they do."

"You may want to have a conversation with her first. She may not be enthused to see you."

"That doesn't matter. We need to stop Esti and her group, or Chi is dead."

"First,"—Monty handed me a steaming cup of Death Wish—"we rest and recover. Then we hunt down your vampire."

THE END

CAST

ANGEL RAMIREZ-DIRECTOR of the NYTF and friend to Simon Strong. Cannot believe how much destruction one detective agency can wage in the course of one day.

Cecil Fairchild-Owner of SuNaTran and close friend of Tristan Montague. Provides transport for the supernatural community and has been known to make a vehicle disappear in record time.

Grey Stryder-one of the last Night Wardens patrolling the city and keeping the streets safe. Current owner of *Kokutan no ken.*

Hades-Ruler of the Underworld. Rules the dead and is generally seen around funerals and wakes. Favorite song by the Eagles is 'Hotel California'-especially that part about checking out, but never leaving.

Kali-(AKA Divine Mother) goddess of Time, Creation, Destruction, and Power. Cursed Simon for unspecified reasons and has been known to hold a grudge. She is also one of the most powerful magic-users in existence.

Karma-The personification of causality, order, and balance. She reaps what you sow. Also known as the mistress of bad timing. Everyone knows the saying karma is a…some days that saying is true.

LD Tush Rogue Creative Mage, husband to TK Tush. Proprietor of Fordey Boutique. One of the Ten.

Michiko Nakatomi-(AKA 'Chi' if you've grown tired of breathing) Vampire leader of the Dark Council. Reputed to be the most powerful vampire in the Council.

Peaches-(AKA Devildog, Hellhound, Arm Shredder and Destroyer of Limbs) Offspring of Cerberus and given to the Montague & Strong Detective Agency to help with their security. Closely resembles a Cane Corso-a very large Cane Corso.

Persephone Goddess of vegetation, wife to Hades, and Ruler of the Underworld. Favorite movie: The Matrix Reloaded, because-"Her character was the best in the film."

Professor Ziller Mage responsible for the safeguarding of the Living Library and the Repository of knowledge at the Golden Circle. Don't try to have conversation with him…it will just melt your brain.

Roxanne DeMarco-Director of Haven. Oversees both the Medical and Detention Centers of the facility. Is an accomplished sorceress with formidable skill. Has been known to make Tristan stammer and stutter with merely a touch of his arm.

Simon Strong-The intelligent (and dashingly handsome) half of the Montague & Strong Detective Agency. Cursed alive into immortality by the goddess

Kali.

TK Tush Rogue Creative Mage, wife to LD Tush. Proprietor of Fordey Boutique. One of the Ten. She's not angry…really.

Tristan Montague- The civilized (and staggeringly brilliant) half of the Montague & Strong Detective Agency. Mage of the Golden Circle sect and currently on 'extended leave' from their ever-watchful supervision.

ORGANIZATIONS

NEW YORK TASK Force-(AKA the NYTF) a quasi-military police force created to deal with any supernatural event occurring in New York City.

SuNaTran-(AKA Supernatural Transportations) Owned by Cecil Fairchild. Provides car and vehicle service to the supernatural community in addition to magic-users who can afford membership.

The Dark Council-Created to maintain the peace between humanity and the supernatural community shortly after the last Supernatural War. Its role is to be a check and balance against another war occurring. Not everyone in the Council favors peace.

#######

Special Mentions for Hell Hath No Fury

Samantha R. Because you can't spell Damage without a Mage.

Chris C II. Because: That building had so many code violations the city was going to close it down (HAHAHAHA). Typical Simon.

The team responsible for renovating the city…one

building at a time.

Carrie Anne: because Peaches can hardly exercise any less LOL [?]!

For the amazing Ode to an Agency found at the front of this book. Thank you Carrie! Stop breaking the games!

Larry and Tammy(WOUF). Even when your characters aren't directly in a story, our regular conversations always influence the feel of the book. It feels like LD & TK are present, ready to step in on a moment's notice. You two are the Watchers of Urban Fantasy!

Glen V. because the **javambrosia** DeathWish Coffee coupon wouldn't exist without you. Thanks to you, we can all… "Stay caffeinated. My friends."

Deathwish Coffee. Because Javambrosia is like a punch in the face from an angel.

AUTHOR NOTES

THANK YOU FOR reading this story and jumping back into the world of Monty & Strong.

Writing this story was quite fun. Anytime I get to showcase Hades, I realize I enjoy myself more than should be proper. This book is a turning point of sorts. The machinations going on behind the scenes are slowly being revealed and of course, Monty & Simon are right in the center.

Simon is starting to grasp more of his role as his bond with Peaches and Ebonsoul deepen. He's headed for a showdown, he just doesn't know with whom or what.

The next book, Reaping Wind takes place in Japan. It picks up right after Hell Hath No Fury (well after Monty and Simon get to rest a bit) and deals primarily with what is happening with Chi and the Blood Hunters.

Reaping Wind will dive a little deeper into the situation with Simon and Chi, the 'relationship' they have, and why Chi gave him Ebonsoul. It also deals with Chi reconciling with her past. I do hope you will jump into that book as Monty & Simon head to the land of the rising sun to stop a group of vampire hunters and a very angry ancient vampire.

With each book, I want to introduce you to different elements of the world Monty & Strong inhabit, slowly revealing who they are and why they make the choices they do. If you want to know how they met, that story is in NO GOD IS SAFE, which is a short, explaining how Tristan and Simon worked their first case.

There are some references you will understand and some…you may not. This may be attributable to my age (I'm older than Monty, or feel that way most mornings) or to my love of all things sci-fi and fantasy. As a reader, I've always enjoyed finding these "Easter Eggs" in the books I read. I hope you do too. If there is a reference you don't get, feel free to email me and I will explain it…maybe.

You will notice that Simon is still a smart-ass (deserving a large head smack) and many times, he's clueless about what's going on. He's also acquired more spells (an anemic magic missile and undead sausage) even though he needs some practice. He's slowly wrapping his head around the world of magic and what it means to be a shieldbearer, but it's a vast universe and he has no map.

Bear with him—he's still new to the immortal, magical world he's been delicately shoved into. Fortunately he has Monty to nudge (or blast) him in the right direction.

Each book will reveal more about Monty & Strong's backgrounds and lives before they met. Rather than hit you with a whole history, I wanted you to learn about them slowly, the way we do with a person we just met—over time (and many large cups of DeathWish Coffee).

Thank you for taking the time to read this book. I wrote it for you and I hope you enjoyed spending a few more hours getting in (and out of) trouble with Tristan and Simon.

If you really enjoyed this story, I need you to do me a **HUGE** favor— **Please leave a review**.

It's really important and helps the book (and me). Plus, it means Peaches gets new titanium chew toys, besides my arms, legs, and assorted furniture to shred. And I get to keep him at normal size (most of the time). He's also thinking of getting Rags some toys and we have to help him impress her. She has very high standards and only the best will do.

We want to help Peaches, don't we?

CONTACT ME:

I REALLY DO appreciate your feedback. Let me know what you thought by emailing me at:
www.orlando@orlandoasanchez.com
For more information on Monty & Strong…come join the MoB Family on Facebook!
You can find us at:
Montague & Strong Case Files.
To get **FREE** stories visit my page at:
www.orlandoasanchez.com

Thank You!

If you enjoyed this book, would you please help me by leaving a review at the site where you purchased it from? It only needs to be a sentence or two and it would really help me out a lot!

All of My Books

The Warriors of the Way

The Karashihan* • Spiritual Warriors • The Ascendants • The Fallen Warrior • The Warrior Ascendant • The Master Warrior

John Kane

The Deepest Cut* • Blur

Sepia Blue

The Last Dance* • Rise of the Night• Sisters• Nightmare

Chronicles of the Modern Mystics

The Dark Flame • A Dream of Ashes

Montague & Strong Detective Agency

Tombyards & Butterflies• Full Moon Howl•Blood Is Thicker• Silver Clouds Dirty Sky • Homecoming• NoGod is Safe•The Date•The War Mage • Dragons&Demigods•Bullets & Blades• A Proper Hellhound

Night Warden

Wander

Brew & Chew Adventures

Hellhound Blues

**Books denoted with an asterisk are FREE via my website.*

www.OrlandoASanchez.com

ART SHREDDERS

No book is the work of just one person. I am fortunate enough to have an excellent team of readers and shredders who give of their time and keen eyes to provide notes, insight, and corrections. They help make this book go from good to great. Each and every one of you helped make this book fantastic.

THANK YOU

Alex P. Amy R. Anne M. Audra V. M. Audrey C. Barbara H. Bennah P. Beverly C. Brandy D. Brenda Nix L. Carrie Anne O. Cassandra H. Chris C II. Claudia L-S. Dana A. Darren M. Davina N. Dawn McQ. M. Denise K. Donna Y H. Hal B. Helen G. Jan G. Jen C. Jim S. Joscelyn S. Joseph M. Julie P. Justin B. Karen H Karen H.

Kirsten B.W. Klaire T. Larry Diaz T. Laura Cadger R. Laura T. LeAnne B. Mary Anne P. MaryAnn S. Marydot H. P. Melody DeL. Mike H. Natalie F. Penny C-M. RC B. Rene C. Rob H. Robert W. Samantha L. Sara Mason B. Shanon O.B. Sharon H. Sondra M. Stacey S. Sue W. Tami C. Tammy Ashwin K. Tehrene H. Terri A. Thomas R. Tracey M.C. Tracy K.Wendy S. Zak K.

ACKNOWLEDGMENTS

I'm finally beginning to understand that each book, each creative expression usually has a large group of people behind it. This story is no different. So let me take a moment to acknowledge my (very large) group:

To my Tribe: You are the reason I have stories to tell. You cannot possibly fathom how much and how deep I love you all.

To Lee: Because you were the first audience I ever had. I love you sis.

To the Logsdon family: JL your support always demands I bring my A-game and produce the best story I can. I always hear: "Don't rush!" in your voice.

L.L. (the Uber Jeditor) your notes and comments turned this story from good to great. I accept the challenge!

Your patience knows no bounds. Thank you both.

Arigatogozaimasu

The Montague & Strong Case Files Group AKA- The MoB(The Mages of BadAssery)

When I wrote T&B there were fifty-five members in The MoB. As of this release there are 957 members in the MoB. I am honored to be able to call you my MoB Family. Thank you for being part of this group and M&S. You each make it possible.

THANK YOU.

WTA-The Incorrigibles

JL,BenZ, EricQK, S.S.,

They sound like a bunch of badass misfits because they are. My exposure to the slightly deranged and extremely deviant brain trust that you are made this book possible. I humbly thank you and…it's all your fault.

The English Advisory

Aaron, Penny, Carrie

For all things English..thank you.

DEATH WISH COFFEE

This book has been powered by DeathWish-Thank you!

Is there any other coffee on the face of the earth or in space that can compare? I think not.

To Deranged Doctor Design

Kim. Darja, Milo

You define professionalism and creativity. Thank you for the great service and amazing covers.

YOU GUYS RULE!

To you the reader:

Thank you for jumping down the rabbit hole with me. I truly hope you enjoy this story. You are the reason I wrote it.

ABOUT THE AUTHOR

Orlando Sanchez has been writing ever since his teens when he was immersed in creating scenarios for playing Dungeon and Dragons with his friends every weekend. An avid reader, his influences are too numerous to list here. Some of the most prominent are: J.R.R. Tolkien, Jim Butcher, Kat Richardson, Terry Pratchett, Christopher Moore,Terry Brooks, Piers Anthony, Lee Child, George Lucas, Andrew Vachss, and Barry Eisler to name a few in no particular order.

The worlds of his books are urban settings with a twist of the paranormal lurking just behind the scenes and generous doses of magic, martial arts, and mayhem.

Aside from writing, he holds a 2nd and 3rd Dan in two distinct styles of Karate. If not training, he is studying some aspect of the martial arts or martial arts philosophy.

Please visit his site at OrlandoASanchez.com for more information about his books and upcoming releases.

Made in the USA
Las Vegas, NV
16 August 2022

53418068R00142